A Corpse in Hut Town

From the Murder on Mars Series

By Greg Fowlkes

Includes a special preview of

The Blood Red Sands of Mars

Book One from the Murder on Mars Series

A Corpse in Hut Town

Published by The Fictional Press

The Fictional Press, an imprint of Intrepid Ink, LLC, provides full publishing services to authors of fiction and non-fiction books, eBooks and websites. From editing to formatting, to publishing, to marketing, Intrepid Ink gets your creative works into the hands of the people who want to read them.

Find out more at www.thefictionalpress.com.

ISBN 13: 978-1-937022-67-9

Printed in the United States of America

Also from the Murder on Mars Series by Greg Fowlkes

The Blood Red Sands of Mars

A Death at Station Alpha

Murder at the Mars Club

Other Books by by Greg Fowlkes

The Fictional Detective

The Laws of Magic

Trial by Magic

Star City Stories

MAPS

Hut Town
and surrounding area

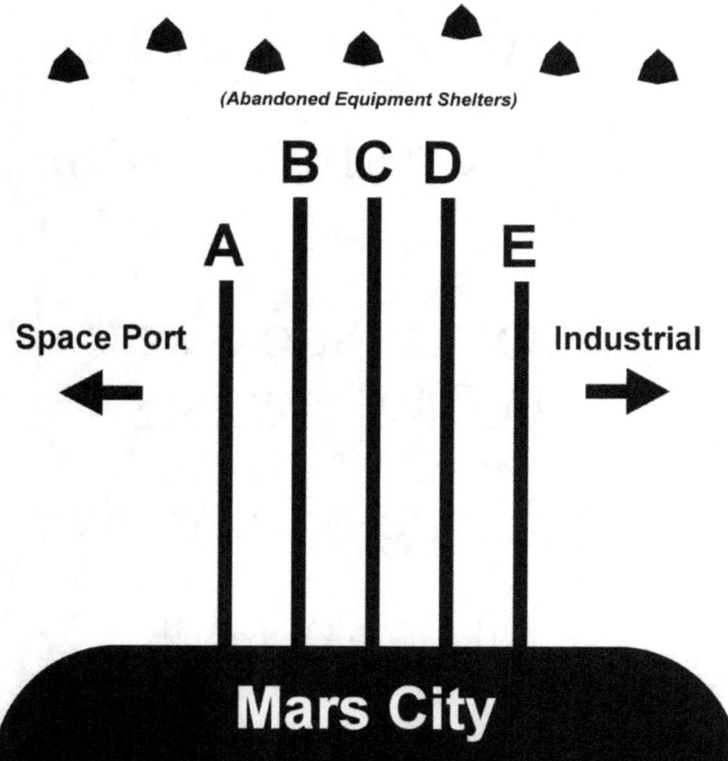
(Abandoned Equipment Shelters)
B C D
A
E
Space Port
Industrial
Mars City

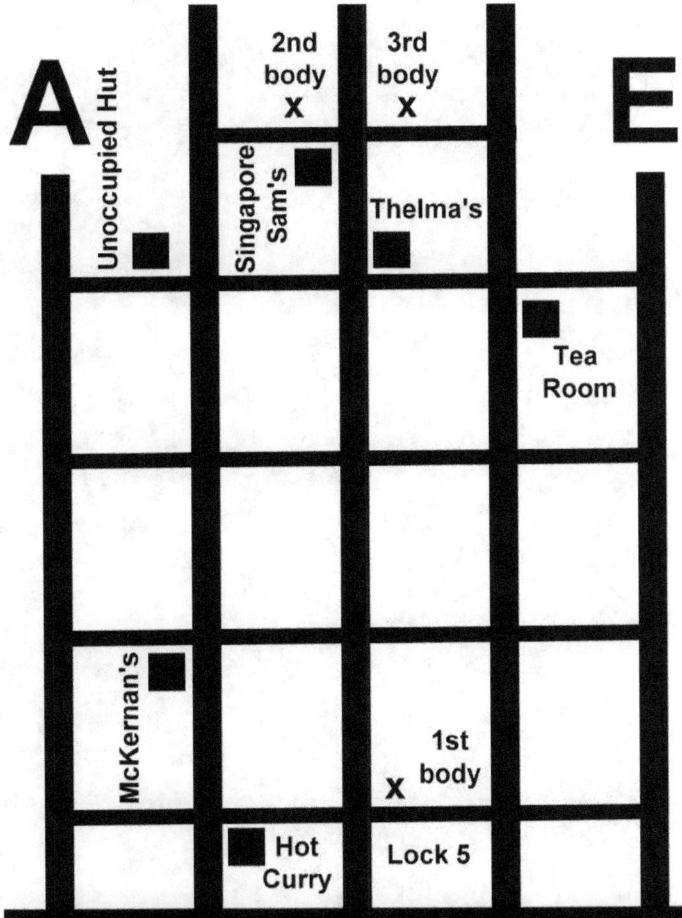
B
C
D
A
E
2nd body
x
3rd body
x
Unoccupied Hut
Singapore Sam's
Thelma's
Tea Room
McKernan's
1st body
x
Hot Curry
Lock 5
Mars City

TABLE OF CONTENTS

Chapter 1: Gaerretts Has a Surprise

McKernan glanced at the clock above his desk and wondered if it was late enough that he could justify leaving to have a beer at Finnegan's. He certainly felt like he needed one. For the last two hours he had been working on the monthly crime statistics report. He knew that no one would ever actually read the report, and even if someone should, no rational action would ever result. Yet each month he was required to compile a list of every fight, assault, robbery, rape and murder on the planet that had been reported to the two dozen men and women under his command. The current Trust Authority governor was even more particular than the last two that the report be completed and filed on schedule. McKernan and the governor did not get along, a fact that didn't concern McKernan in the least.

McKernan was saved from further rumination on this situation by the buzzing of his communicator. A glance at the display showed that it was Gaeretts, the oldest man on the force and his number two. Given the staffing levels of the Martian constabulary, that didn't excuse him from taking patrol, though it did allow him to pick his shift.

"McKernan here. What is it?"

"Chief, there's something you need to see." Gaeretts had a tendency to be less than deferential to his superior. As he was the man McKernan trusted most to protect his back, he was willing to let that slide.

"What?"

"I'd rather you see for yourself. I'm in the utilities tunnel in Corridor C just past Lock 5."

McKernan sighed. He was really feeling the need for that beer, but Gaeretts was anything but an alarmist. If he thought there was something that needed his attention, then it did.

"I'll be there in fifteen minutes."

"I'll be here. Bring a crime scene kit."

That didn't sound good. Mars didn't have a separate forensics squad. With most of the crime consisting of fights between miners in town for a bender, there really wasn't much need for one. The kit consisted mostly of a camera to take photos, supplies to take fingerprints, latex gloves, and bags for evidence. He grabbed the bag containing the kit from the cabinet where it was stored and headed out.

Two years ago the jail and police offices had moved from their old location in two of the original Mars base huts into new quarters in the core part of Mars City. They were still anything but luxurious, but at least the walls were silica brick instead of aluminum foil and sprayed on foam and there was a solid roof overhead. The new location was in the latest addition, mostly reserved for the less important Trust Authority departments.

Corridor C, on the other hand, was part of Hut Town, that relic from the original base where the construction consisted of inflatable structures of aluminum foil, sprayed on insulated foam and not much else. The Trust Authority services and the major corporations had long ago migrated into the more substantial confines of Mars City while Hut

Town had been taken over by entrepreneurs, small companies and anyone else looking for more room and lower rents. It also was home to most of the saloons, brothels and other establishments catering to miners and prospectors in town to blow off steam.

Somewhere along the line Hut Town had become capitalized. The population was nearly balanced between Mars City proper and Hut Town, and between the two they contained nearly a fifth of the population of the entire planet. How much authority the Trust had in Hut Town was an open question subject to interpretation on a case by case basis.

The airlock to Corridor C was on the other side of Mars City from the police office, which was about a ten minute walk. McKernan took it briskly, too familiar with the sights to pay attention. A few of those he passed by waved. Everybody on Mars knew who he was, but it was mostly the old timers, those who had been on Mars for more than a few years, who acknowledged the fact.

Periodically he passed through airlocks, though in Mars City they were left open unless there was an emergency. The walls and ceiling here were of silica blocks. Halfway through the city he came to the main corridor, now officially named "The Concourse." This was a broad expanse twenty meters wide and ten high that extended for several hundred meters in either direction. This was where the Mars Hotel and the Sheraton were located and the major corporations kept their facades. It was also where the "important" Trust Authority offices were centered.

Attempts had been made to dress up the space with potted shrubs and small trees stuck in containers, Overhead a scattering of skylights let in shafts of natural lights. But the walls were still made of unpainted silica blocks and the floor was paved in tiles of the same substance, slightly roughened to provide traction. The effect was like nothing so much as a rather dismal suburban shopping mall.

McKernan strode across the empty space quickly. Like most Martians, open spaces made him nervous unless he was wearing a surface suit. On the far side he entered the corridor that led to Corridor C. A hundred meters farther along he came to the first airlock that was closed. Hut Town lay on the other side.

Corridor C, at least the near end of it, was mostly occupied by small businesses, those selling goods and services. Much of it was geared to the independent prospectors and miners that roamed the face of Mars looking for rare earths and other ores worth sending back to Earth. Increasingly though, much of the commerce was aimed at other residents of Hut Town, those who didn't live in the Trust Authority or corporate dormitories and apartments.

McKernan pressed the button that opened the lock, stepped inside, and hit the control to close it. Once the inner door closed there was a brief moment while the pressure equalized to the corridor beyond, and then the outer door opened. The corridors of Hut Town were kept at a lower pressure than Mars City. They were also a lot colder. The Trust didn't pay to heat them. Or provide any services to Hut Town, for that matter. Those were up to the residents to provide. The Trust Authority's attitude towards Hut Town could be summed up as "benign neglect." Mars couldn't survive without the people that lived and worked there, but that didn't mean they had to be encouraged.

Unlike the passageways that he had been traversing, here the corridor consisted of a nearly circular tube some five meters in diameter. The walls were of unfinished foam, with a thin skin of aluminum on the outside to keep in the air. Along the walls ran various pipes and conduits, and McKernan knew that below the corrugated metal floor there was a space with more utilities. Lighting was provided by dim fixtures at wide intervals. More illumination was provided by the signs above the airlocks that penetrated the sides of the corridor. These marked the locations of the various businesses along the corridor. All these locks were closed. In Hut Town you didn't take any chances.

A hundred meters along the corridor he came to another airlock. This was lock 3. The first one he had gone through was lock 2. Lock 1 had disappeared in a previous expansion of Mars City. Those residents of Hut Town who had been displaced had not been happy, but they hadn't had much say. The Trust Authority had the final word, and as it drew its powers from the U.N. on Earth and the corporations, it tended to ignore people on Mars.

McKernan cycled through the lock and the next two beyond it. Once past lock 5 he saw that an access hatch was open in the floor just beyond it. Gaeretts and a man he recognized as working for the power utility were standing over the open hatch.

"So what is it that you had to drag me out here for?" McKernan asked.

Gaeretts was about ten years older than McKernan, his sparse hair turning gray. He had the wiry build of most long term Martians. He was dressed in what passed for the official uniform of a constable and there were sergeant's stripes on his sleeve.

"Down there," he said plainly.

McKernan took a look down the hatch. Gaeretts shown his flash down the hole. There was a body. It looked to be that of a young woman. She was wearing skimpy dress completely unsuitable for the temperature in the corridor.

From the desiccated condition of the body, it was clear the body had been there some time.

"You found the body?" McKernan asked the man with Gaeretts.

"Yeah. There'd been a complaint about one of the power feeds. I came down to check it out. When I opened up the hatch to climb down, I saw the body. Gave me a shock. I guess I didn't move for a couple of minutes. That's when Gaeretts came along."

"I was doing my rounds. I'd just taken the cross corridor from B. When I saw this guy standing with his mouth open I knew something was up. It didn't take more than one look to tell me what. I called you."

"You didn't go down? Neither one of you?"

"I know my business, Chief," Gaeretts answered. The utility man just shook his head.

"OK. Here's the kit. Take a few pictures before we go down."

While he worked the camera, McKernan interviewed the man who discovered the body.

"What's your name?"

"Flint. Jim Flint." He flashed the ID dangling from a cord around his neck but McKernan ignored that.

"Don't suppose you recognize the girl?"

"No. I never saw her before in my life."

"I didn't think you would. Any idea when the last time someone was in that tunnel?"

"Hard to say. No one from Power has been down there for years. I can't tell you about other departments. But the only time anyone goes down in the tunnels is when something's broke."

"Yeah, and from the look of the dust down there it doesn't look like anyone else has been there for years, either."

"Look, can I go now?" Flint asked. I got other work I need to do." From the look of him, he wanted to get as far away from that tunnel as he could. Bodies will do that to some people, McKernan thought.

"Sure. You can go. I know where to find you," McKernan replied. On Mars there really wasn't anywhere to go. "And let us know if you find any more bodies."

"You really think there could be more down there?" Flint asked.

"No."

CHAPTER 2: THE BODY IN THE TUNNEL

After Flint left, McKernan climbed down the access ladder into the tunnel taking care not to disturb the body. He'd never liked dealing with corpses though he'd seen enough of them in his life. The tunnel, which was the bottom half of the cylinder that formed the corridor, was low with hardly enough room for the average man to stand up in. On either side of the center walkway were pipes and conduits hemming it in on either side so that there was only about a meter of free space. There was no illumination except for his flash and the light that bounced in through the access hatch.

He directed his light up and down the tunnel. Though the dust lay a centimeter thick there were no signs of footprints as far as his flash could reach. Flint was right, no one had been in this section of tunnel for a long time, maybe years. There was a coating of dust on the body as well.

He took a close look at the corpse. It appeared to be that of a young woman. It was impossible to judge the age with any degree of certainty. The cold, dry air in the corridor had desiccated the body until it was practically a mummy. She had short, blonde hair which looked as if it had been dyed by an amateur. That wasn't surprising. He didn't know of any beauty salons on Mars. Discounting the mummification, the body still looked painfully thin. She had been flat-chested as well. There were traces of cosmetics on the face and a red polish on the nails. That was unusual as both were scarce on Mars due to the expense of shipping them from Earth.

She was wearing a short, sleeveless dress of a thin fabric. He couldn't see any signs of undergarments through the dress. She wasn't wearing any stockings or tights either. There were no signs of shoes or a handbag. She certainly didn't look as if she were dressed for roaming around corridors where the temperature was only a few degrees above freezing.

There were no obvious wounds, no signs of a struggle. It wasn't clear to McKernan whether the fact that the body was curled up into a fetal position was due to the actions of the woman before death or the process of desiccation.

"You want me to come down yet, Chief?" Gaerretts called from above.

"You might as well. Take some close ups of the body and shots up and down the tunnel. And try not to disturb the dust any more than you have to."

Gaerretts came down with the camera. It was dark enough that he had to use a flash. McKernan looked away studying lengths of the tunnel.

After he was done with the pictures McKernan asked, "Recognize her?" The sergeant patrolled the seedier side of Hut Town more often than he did. If anyone was likely to know her it was Gaerretts.

"Hard to tell, dried out like that, but I don't think so. She's not one of the regular working girls."

"Think she was working freelance? That was why she ended up here?" McKernan queried.

"Naw. If anything, they'd try to recruit her. Young talent is scarce on Mars." Gaerretts could be cynical at times. McKernan knew that he was also probably right. The male-to-female ratio on Mars was about six-to-one. Any honest woman could have her choice of suitors. Even the prostitutes could be selective if they were so inclined. Competitive pressure kept the sex business reasonably honest.

"Any ideas?"

"I don't know. Dressed like that maybe she was going to a party or on a date and it went wrong."

"Do we have any missing persons reports on file that fit the description?" McKernan asked.

"On Mars? It's damned hard to go missing in Mars City. It's not even that easy out in the boonies unless you're stupid or trying to get lost."

"Better check the reports anyway," McKernan said.

"OK, Chief. What do you say? About 160 centimeters and 50 kilos?"

"About that. Might not be blonde. The dye job looks like it might have been done shortly before she was killed."

Gaerretts played around with his communicator for a few minutes.

"The only missing person we got is a guy that cheated a couple of miners in a crooked card game. He's either hiding out or buried out in the dunes. No women have gone missing."

"I didn't think so. You see anything I don't?"

"I see a dead girl who looks like she's been lying there for months. No tracks, no wounds, nothing to identify her. Maybe she just fell through the hatch and broke her neck. Or knocked herself out and froze to death."

"That's a pleasant thought."

"So what do we do now, Chief?"

"Take her to the hospital. Let one of the docs do an autopsy. Maybe a tox screen."

"You thinking drugs?"

"Maybe. We've had amateur pharmacists before."

Gaerretts just grunted. "How do we get her out?"

"She shouldn't be that hard to move. I think Ferris is on duty at the station. Give him a call and tell him to get a hold of some kind of cart we can put the body on. And tell him to bring a sheet. I don't want to be wheeling a corpse through Mars City."

Gaerretts conducted a short conversation on his communicator. "He'll be here in fifteen minutes or so."

The body proved harder to move than they thought. It wasn't that heavy, but it wouldn't unfold from the fetal position. The access hatch was less than a half meter in diameter. In the end, they had to wait till Ferris showed up and hand the corpse up to him while he maneuvered it through the opening from above.

Chapter 3: The Doctor in the House

After they got the body loaded onto the cart Ferris had brought, McKernan sent Gaerretts to mind the station. He let Ferris push the cart, only helping to get it through the airlocks. The younger constable didn't seem to mind.

What passed for the only hospital on Mars was a set of rooms carved out of the original Trust building. There were only a dozen doctors on the planet, the eight that worked for the Trust Authority at the hospital in Mars City and another four that worked for various mining corporations at the larger camps spread around the globe. An equal number of physician's assistants and a score of nurses pretty much made up the planet's pool of medical talent. There wasn't much in the way of communicable disease on Mars, and with the health screening required of contract workers and Trust staff, congenital problems were fairly rare. The population of Mars was for the most part under fifty and, due to the expense of shipping food, ate a diet high in vegetables and low in animal fat. Accidents formed the bulk of medical problems, and on Mars you were more likely to die from an accident than require medical attention.

The nurse on duty at the front desk looked up as they entered, and seeing the cloth draped body on the cart just motioned them through the doors leading to the surgery.

"Dr. Haestert is the doctor on duty," he added as they pushed their way through the swinging doors.

Elisabeth Haestert was a thin woman of medium height in her mid thirties. Her straight blonde hair was pulled back into a pony tail, and she was wearing the traditional scrubs. She was a relative newcomer to Mars, still in the first year of her three year contract with the Trust Authority. McKernan had met her once or twice but hadn't had to deal with her on a professional basis.

"What can I do for you, Inspector?" she asked looking up from the computer tablet she had been staring at.

"I've got a body here," McKernan answered tersely.

"I can see that," the doctor responded sarcastically. "Not much I can do about that, I'm afraid."

"I need to know how she died and when, if at all possible. I also need to know who she was."

"You don't know?" Haestert asked, her interest aroused. There weren't all that many people on Mars, and most carried some form of ID with them.

McKernan related the details of how and where the body was found.

"I'll do my best, but I'm no pathologist, Inspector. There isn't one on Mars as far as I know."

"Yeah, I know," McKernan responded. "Do your best. Right now I'm operating in the dark. I don't know whether I'm dealing with an accident or if there's a murderer running loose."

"Oh, well. I was bored anyway. Things have been slow. It will be an interesting diversion. I can probably let you know the basics in a couple of hours. A tox screen and lab work will take more time, but I can draw the samples at least."

"Thanks, doc. You can reach me on my communicator. If not, just call the station."

"I'll let you know when I have something."

As McKernan turned to leave, the doctor's gaze followed him. The inspector had acquired something of a reputation in his six years on Mars. There weren't many who would willingly go up against him from what she had heard. There were stories of a shoot out some years back that had left a number of men dead and one of the big mining companies banned from the planet. In person, he seemed less mythic, but there was a certain lean toughness about him that he had in common with many of the older Mars hands she came across.

After leaving the hospital McKernan headed back to the station. He still had his reports to finish, though his mind was more preoccupied with the body they had found. It was a pleasant surprise, then that he noted the short Hispanic woman sitting in a chair across from Gaerretts' desk.

"Constable Ortiz," he said with a smile. "I thought you'd be taking it easy at Junction 3. I hope there's nothing wrong."

"No, everything's fine," Ortiz replied. "It's just that the doctor wants me to stay in Mars City for the last couple of months before the baby is born." She patted her belly self-consciously. Constable Elena Ortiz's normal beat was patrolling a thousand kilometer stretch of roadway centered around a small settlement named Junction 3. "There haven't been that many pregnancies brought to term on Mars, and the effects of low gravity concern her. Out at Junction 3 it would be more than a day before I could get into Mars City or someone could get out there."

"They probably know best," McKernan replied, somewhat uncomfortably. Ortiz was one of only two women on his small force. He had worked with her on the case at Station Alpha, and knew she was both competent and reliable. But talking about pregnancies and babies was something he rarely did.

"They're probably just covering their asses," Ortiz stated. Before coming to Mars, Ortiz had served a stint as a policeman in the Air Force, and was treating her pregnancy much more matter-of-factly than her colleagues.

"So what are you doing here? I'd think you'd be taking advantage of the vacation."

"I'm bored out of my mind. Mike is still back at Junction 3 running the business. With a baby on the way we can use all the money we can get. I've never been one much for reading or watching videos. And sitting alone in a small room in the Trust quarters isn't my idea of fun. I thought there might be something for me to do around here until the baby comes."

"I think we've pretty well got things covered. It's been quiet the last few months," McKernan responded.

"Anything, Chief. I'm desperate. I'll even do reports," Ortiz pleaded.

"You know, boss," Gaeretts interjected, "Ortiz could man the front desk. That would free up me or Ferris if we need to do some investigating of this murder."

"Murder?" Ortiz pricked up.

"We don't even know if it's a murder yet," McKernan objected.

"The body of a young woman was found out in one of the tunnels in Hut Town," Gaeretts explained.

"Sounds like you might need some help, Chief," Ortiz said.

"Ok. I'll keep it in mind. I guess there isn't any harm in you sitting around manning the phones and looking pretty," McKernan said with a grin. Ortiz was a good cop but anything but a looker.

"Thanks, Chief."

"Just make sure that its cleared with the doc," McKernan said before heading to his cubby hole of an office.

Chapter 4: What the Doctor Discovered

Two hours later, McKernan had finally finished and posted his report. He was sitting back thinking about a drink at Finnegan's when his communicator rang. A quick glance at the display showed it was Dr. Haestert.

"McKernan here. You got something for me, Doc?"

"Inspector. I've completed my preliminary examination of the body. There are several things you need to know," the doctor said.

"What? Have you identified the body?"

"No. But I do have a cause of death."

"So?"

"I think it would be better if I went over my findings in person. Can you come to the surgery?"

"You're being mysterious, Doc. But I can be there in five minutes."

"I'll be waiting," Haestert said before hanging up.

As he walked towards the hospital, McKernan pondered the doctor's call. She had certainly been cryptic. Haestert hadn't struck him as the melodramatic type.

Once at the hospital, he went past the front desk with a wave and through the doors into the surgery.

"What's the story, Doc? You said you knew how she died?"

"Hello to you too, Inspector," the doctor said with a trace of annoyance. "I took some X-rays, and I think I've established the cause of death. I'm pretty sure he was strangled."

"Strangled?" McKernan responded, and then, "Did you say he?"

"Yes. Your victim is a young male. I'd say about twenty. There are signs in the X-ray of the tissue around the throat being crushed. I'm no expert in these matters, but I'd say it was done by someone with very strong hands."

"Wait a minute, Doc. Are you sure? About the sex of the victim, I mean?"

"I admit I'm no forensic pathologist, Inspector, but they did teach us the difference between boys and girls in medical school. It was pretty obvious once I had removed the victim's clothing."

"Sorry, Doc. I didn't mean to question you. I'm just surprised."

"I can understand your confusion, Inspector. It's quite clear that the victim was trying to appear to be woman, and in fact had been taking steps in that direction for some time. There's evidence that he had undergone treatments to have his facial hair removed permanently. He's also had some plastic surgery done along those lines. Not to mention the hair and makeup. Of course, the depilation and plastic surgery may not mean he had gender identity issues. There are parts of the world where they are not that uncommon."

"Have you been able to establish his identity?"

"No, surprisingly not. You'd think that with the small number of people on Mars it wouldn't be a problem, but there was really nothing on the body to give us an ID. The biometrics don't match anyone in the registry."

"Nothing in the clothing?" McKernan asked.

"The dress has a label, but it's a cheap line sold on Earth. I'm pretty sure that neither the UN commissary or any of the local stores sold it. Clothing options on Mars tend to be more… utilitarian shall we say. I recognize the panties as a brand sold locally, but I suspect that it would be impossible to trace the buyer. He wasn't wearing anything else."

"No bra?" McKernan asked.

"Surprisingly, no. You'd think that a man trying to impersonate a woman would wear one, wouldn't you. But I'm pretty sure he wasn't wearing one at the time he was killed."

"Any chance the hair dye and dress were put on after death?"

"I can't say for sure about the dress, though I doubt it. As to the dye job, I would say that was done two or three weeks before death. Dark roots are starting to show."

"I've got to ask this," McKernan said. "Was there any sign of sexual intercourse?"

"No. No signs of anal penetration. No traces of semen, either. There are signs of bruising on the arms. Again, they indicate someone with strong hands."

"OK. So we have a young man, a boy practically, wearing a dress who was probably roughed up and then strangled. I don't suppose you can give me a time of death?"

"Your joking, Inspector? Right?"

"I'm not expecting miracles, Doc. Even the nearest month would be helpful."

"As I've said, I've had no formal training in forensic pathology. I'm your basic general practitioner. But from what little I know about the subject and from what I assume were the conditions in the tunnel where he was found, we're probably talking years, not months. It takes a long time for a body to mummify naturally. I can send an enquiry to experts on Earth if you'd like?"

"Yes, do that, Doc. Please," McKernan said, deciding that the doctor really was trying to be helpful.

"What about fingerprints?"

"The fingers have been pretty well shriveled up by the cold. If this were Earth, there might be things that could be done, but I'm afraid that we have neither the facilities or expertise here on Mars."

"DNA?"

"Again, we don't have the facilities. There really isn't much call for DNA analysis on Mars. Everybody is supposed to have DNA samples taken on Earth before they come here, so we can just consult their medical records if we need to know something. So there's no need to do it locally. And it's not just the analyzer that's a problem. It's all the specialized reagents that are needed for the process. We've just never seen the need to put it in the budget. After all, there are things we need a lot worse. I can take samples and send them to Earth, but you probably know the current transit time better than I do."

McKernan did. Depending on the relative orbital positions of Mars and the Earth it took anywhere from a month to two hundred days to make the trip. That was one of the things that made shipping things between the two planets so expensive.

"Go ahead and do it, Doc," McKernan said.

"Shipping will have to come out of your budget, not the hospital's."

"I'll authorize it. What about drugs?"

"A tox screen we can do. We do have access to a mass spectrometer and can certainly run tests for any of the drugs that are readily available on Mars. I've already taken samples for those. They'll probably be run in the morning. I should have the results for you by tomorrow afternoon at the latest."

"Thanks, Doc. Anything else you can tell me that might be of use?"

"Well, I'm pretty sure that our victim didn't die immediately after he was strangled. There are signs of damage from exposure that could only occur while he was alive."

"So what you're saying is that the murderer choked this kid and then stuffed him down that tunnel while he was still alive to freeze to death."

"That's about the size of it, Inspector. I hope you catch the bastard."

"So do I. Thanks, Doc. You've been a big help under the circumstances."

"What do you want us to do with the body?"

"You've got storage facilities here, don't you? That will preserve the bodies condition?"

"No problem. If there's one thing Mars has got plenty of it's cold and dry. If there's nothing else, my shift ended about an hour ago. I'd like to go home and take a nice hot shower. Of course, on Mars that's not likely to happen."

"Sorry to keep you, Doc," McKernan said. Then, almost as an afterthought, "I was about to go for a drink at Finnegan's when you called. Would you care to join me?"

The doctor looked at the inspector for a moment, then shrugged and said, "Why not?"

Chapter 5: Drinks at Finnegan's

Finnegan's is one of Mars' great mysteries. It's a quiet little bar located right on the main corridor halfway between the Mars Sheraton and the Mars Hotel. It's dark, has no juke box, and the video screen behind the bar usually operates only to show football matches on Sunday afternoons. Sometimes the football is American style and sometimes not. It doesn't really matter, all the games are recordings. With a day forty minutes longer and a year nearly twice as long as Earth, the daily cycle on Mars has long lost any synchronization with the home planet. The important thing is that Finnegan's has a real mahogany bar stretching the length of one wall and only serves decent booze, not the industrial alcohol with artificial flavoring and coloring that is served everywhere else on Mars except for the cocktail lounge at the Mars Sheraton and the restaurant in the Mars Hotel. How and where Finnegan procures his spirits is part of the mystery.

The other part of the mystery is Finnegan himself, the eponymous proprietor of the establishment. No one can figure out what he is doing on Mars or why he is running a bar. Many have asked him, but he steadfastly refuses to give anything but nonsensical answers such as "he's there for the climate." It certainly can't be to get rich. Presumably Finnegan's makes a profit, but it is hard to see how. His prices, compared to his competition, are not only fair, but downright cheap. Considering the shipping costs on a fifth of Scotch, it's hard to understand how he didn't go broke years ago. There were rumors that various people involved in the space trade owed him favors. Of course there were also rumors that Finnegan owned half the shares of Anglo Martian mining, as well. McKernan had learned long ago to discount rumors.

In a serious breach of protocol, the inspector, driven by curiosity, had looked into Finnegan's personnel file, that dossier the Trust Authority kept on every person resident on the planet. It had been singularly uninformative. Colin Finnegan was a citizen of The Irish Republic, having been born in Macroom some sixty five years earlier. He had come to Mars as a "special consultant" to the Trust Authority at about the time the first portions of the official Mars City were being built. At the end of his contract, instead of returning to Earth, he had cashed out and bought the portion of the new city that was to become the bar. He had paid a ridiculously low price by current standards, but Mars had been a much different place back then, all of a decade earlier. The reason given for his remaining on Mars was "for his health." It was possible. The lower gravity on Mars made life easier for some people with heart conditions. For some, returning to Earth after an extended period on Mars was impossible.

For whatever reason, by whatever means, Finnegan ran his bar, and ran it the way he saw fit. He was selective about his clientele, the main criteria seeming to be paying your bill and minding your manners while within the confines of the establishment. No fights, no loud arguments, no annoying political discussions. Violate one of these rules and one would find service painfully slow or nonexistent. A slight exception was made during the football game on Sunday when one was allowed to root for the "home team" and disparage the referees. Not surprisingly, the patrons of Finnegan's tended to be the older, more responsible, and longer term residents of Mars, tending more towards the midlevel staff of the Trust Authority and mining conglomerates than towards miners and prospectors in town for a spree. Everyone seemed to like it that way.

When McKernan and the doctor entered, the place was fairly empty and they had no problem finding a table along the wall opposite the bar. Finnegan was at his usual place behind the bar. McKernan had never been there during business hours when he had not been on the premises, though on occasion, as on football Sundays, he might have a part time helper.

"What can I get you, Doc?" McKernan asked.

"For one, you can stop calling me Doc, Inspector."

"What can I call you, then?"

"My friends call me Beth," the doctor answered.

"Am I a friend?"

"For the moment."

"Then what would you like, Beth?"

"You know I haven't had a decent glass of wine since I came to Mars. Do they have one here?"

"If they have it anywhere, it will be here. Any preference?"

"Anything as long as it's red," the doctor answered with a smile.

McKernan made his way to the bar. There was a moment of consultation with the proprietor. A glass and a bottle were produced, the glass filled with a certain ceremony. Finnegan seemed to be enjoying himself. The inspector ordered a Scotch, neat, with water on the side for himself.

"Finnegan said it's a petite sirah from Sonoma. He also said to be careful with the glass, he's running low. By the way, you can call me Erik."

"Thank you, Erik." The smile was becoming a habit.

They sat in silence for a moment sipping their drinks.

"How's the wine?"

"Actually quite good. Finnegan seems to know his wines."

"Not surprising. He seems to know something about everything."

After another silence Beth asked, "You've been on Mars a while, haven't you?"

"Yes, I'm about a year into my third three year contract with the Authority."

"You must like it here, then."

"I'm used to it. It beats my options back on Earth."

"Have you any plans for going back?"

"I don't know. I had a conversation a while back with a man who'd been on Mars longer than anyone. He said I had to be careful. You could reach a point where you couldn't go back. He was talking about the body, about becoming adjusted to the lower gravity. But I think he meant more than that. I just can't see myself back in someplace like SoCal where I grew up. I kind of like the freedom I have here, and most of the people, too. What about you? How are you liking it? You've been here nearly a year?"

"Have you been checking up on me?" the doctor asked warily.

"It's my business to know things. But, no, I haven't been checking up on you. It's just that Mars is a small place, and someone like a new doctor gets noticed."

"Oh. I don't know. To tell the truth, I haven't seen much of Mars outside the hospital. I haven't really even been out on the surface yet."

"I'll have to take you sometime. There are places that can be really beautiful. So why did you come to Mars?"

"Usual story, I suppose. I graduated from Med school owing a lot of money. I found that there were a lot more young doctors than there were positions. I worked temporary assignments for three years not getting anywhere. Then I saw a posting from the Trust Authority. Three years on Mars and they would pay off all my student loans. Meanwhile, my living expenses would be taken care of and I'd be paid a healthy salary besides. It seemed a dream. I applied, was accepted, went through the space training and here I am."

"And?"

"Oh, medically it's not bad. Martians tend to be pretty healthy people. It's mostly minor accidents. I admit that the conditions are a bit spartan, but really no worse than what I put up with in med school."

"But?"

"Well, I find it kind of lonely."

"I can't believe that. With men outnumbering women six or seven to one you must get plenty of attention."

"Attention I can do without in most cases. No, it's that I just don't seem to be making any friends. It's like all of the staff at the hospital, they're here for their three years and then they're going home, so no one is bothering to form any attachments."

"You should get out more."

"Maybe I should."

There was another moment of silence, then the doctor said, "Let's not talk about me. What about you?"

"What do you want to know?"

She thought about it for a moment. "Well, what about the titles. You're the Chief Inspector, the people under you are constables. It's like something out of an old British mystery."

McKernan laughed. "There's a lot to that. When they were setting up the security force it was all done by a committee back on Earth. A lot of the members were diplomats from third world countries. They wanted to avoid any hint of military ranks. Sheriff or Marshall were seen as too American. Commissar was out as too Soviet. Inspector and Constable were seen as relatively neutral. Also, I think at least one of the committee members was a fan of old mysteries. No one else had a better idea. By the way, I didn't become Chief Inspector until I signed my second contract."

"So, do you have many mysteries to solve?"

"No, not really. Most of the crime we have to deal with is fights between miners in town on a spree or petty theft. No thefts of emerald necklaces. Not much in the way of murder. This latest case may be the most mysterious I've had to deal with. But let's not talk shop. Can I get you another drink?"

She checked her communicator for the time. "I'd love to, but I think I'd better get going. But I'd like to, some other time if you'd like," she said shyly.

"It would be my pleasure," McKernan said rising as she left.

After she'd gone, he thought about another drink, but decided against it.

CHAPTER 6: HOME SUITE HOME

Leaving Finnegan's, McKernan walked down the length of the main corridor of Mars City. At this time of night—it was 20:00 hours—it was fairly empty, with only a few pedestrians wandering its length, most of them moving as if they were in a hurry to get to their destinations. The shops and offices that lined the sides of the space were mostly dark. Not for the first time, the detective had the depressing thought that the concourse resembled nothing so much as an aging shopping mall back on Earth.

Reaching a side passage towards the far end he stepped through an open airtight door into a much smaller corridor and headed north. The lighting along its length was more subdued. The closed hatches of various offices and businesses stood along either side, each marked with a sign, more or less discrete, depending on the nature of the enterprise within. Having passed this way every day, he was familiar with each of them.

A hundred meters down the side corridor he came to the airlock that marked the border between Mars City and Hut Town. Unlike the door at the other end, this one was closed. He pushed the button to cycle the lock and stepped through. The inner door closed behind him and the farther door opened, only to close behind him once he had stepped through.

The new section, part of the respectable commercial portion of Hut Town, had less of a finished appearance to it. It's pneumatic origins as part of the original settlement were more visible. The air was cooler and drier, though still not unpleasant. This length of corridor was buried under sand which provided some insulation and protection from radiation. McKernan continued his journey.

After the next lock, the floor sloped upward in front of him. It was a gentle slope, but it still indicated that the tunnel was leaving the subterranean realm of Mars City. The air was crisp, but not quite clean, with the lingering odors of lubricants and decades of humanity.

He passed through several more locks before reaching the final length of corridor before his destination. This last had a marked difference from the those he had passed through before. For one thing, it was clean. An effort had been made to sweep up the dust that seemed to get everywhere. It was also better lit and warmer. He was in one of the better residential sections of Hut Town. The resident's committee had undertaken certain improvements and arranged for periodic maintenance. That they had no authority under the Trust agreements to do so was of little concern. As with much of what went on in Hut Town, they did what they could get away with.

McKernan stopped before one of the airlock hatches that lined the corridor. He withdrew a key from his pocket and inserted it in the mechanical lock warding the hatch mechanism. He turned the key and opened the hatch stepping through into the tiny chamber within. Out of habit, he checked the gauge to make sure there was pressure on the far side. Reassured that there was, he closed the corridor hatch and opened the interior one. Reaching around to the side he flicked a switch to turn on the lights. He was home.

Six months into his first three year contract, McKernan had tired of the tiny room that had been assigned him in the Trust Authority's bachelor quarters. He had found one of the huts for sale by an engineer returning to Earth. At the time, those inflatable relicts of the early days of Martian settlement had been the only option to the tightly controlled confines of Mars City. The Trust Authority kept promising to build private apartments and residential condos, but somehow they never did.

The eight by fifteen meter hut had been spacious compared to the room in the Trust quarters. There had been, of course, a down side. The hut was old, and much of the life support machinery was worn out. The first few years had been a constant battle of scrounging for parts and making connections to those who could fix things. Being on his own, he had been responsible for his oxygen and water, which had been an expense. On the other side of the equation, like most of the residents in Hut Town, he grew plants both for food and oxygen. He sold the surplus back to the Authority, as well as the methane generated by his compost vessel. Eventually, after some improvements, at the end of the month he was not only breaking even, he was making a small profit.

Along with his salary and his unused housing allowance, he had built up a bit of a nest egg, some of which went back into improving the hut with added insulation and other amenities. His big opportunity had come a little over a year earlier when his next door neighbor had taken a position at a mining operation on the far side of the planet. He had sold McKernan his hut at a reasonable price. A salvaged airlock had been spliced in between the two units. The result had left him with not only more space, but separate bedroom and living-room/kitchen areas. He had become the envy of the corridor.

There were still things to do, of course. One of the ideas being put forth by the resident's committee was to erect silica block walls between the huts, roof them over and bury the whole corridor. It would be expensive, but in the long run it would save energy and offer additional protection against radiation above that provided by the limited amount of shielding in the hut ceilings.

Automatically, McKernan went through the routine of making sure that the plants that took up much of the far end of the hut had enough water, that the composter was working, and that the batch of beer he had brewing in a recycled air tank was doing ok. Assured that everything was fine, he thought about having a drink, but decided he wasn't in the mood.

He settled on dinner, some leftover stew and the remains of a container of takeout from the oriental restaurant that operated in the next length of corridor. While these were reheating on the burners of his cook-top, he checked his e-mail and the news feeds, but there was nothing requiring his attention. There was no mention of the corpse they'd found on the Trust Authority's news channel, which wasn't surprising. What news there was ran to the most recent mine openings and the Authority's promises of a better tomorrow. The local Hut Town channel, a mostly amateur production, had a brief mention along with a video of Gaeretts saying "no comment," as only the sergeant could do.

He finished his meal, washed up, and then for lack of anything better to do, went to bed.

Chapter 7: The Investigation is Launched

When McKernan arrived at the police offices he found Ortiz ensconced behind the front desk while Gaeretts was holding a coffee cup. The two had evidently been discussing what details they knew about the body found in Corridor C.

"So, Chief, what did the Doc have to say?"

"The doctor," McKernan found he had to stop himself from referring to her as Beth, "gave me the preliminaries last night. Some details, such as the toxicology results, will have to wait till the tests are run, but it appears we have ourselves a murder."

Gaeretts gave out a low whistle. Ortiz just asked, "So who was the victim?"

"The identity of the victim is, as yet, unknown. What the doctor could tell me is that the victim was a white male in his early twenties. The immediate cause of death appears to have been exposure, but he had been strangled before death. There was bruising and damage to cartilage in the throat area. It seems probable that the victim was rendered unconscious and dumped in the tunnel underneath Corridor C."

"Excuse me, Chief, but did you say 'male'?" Gaeretts asked.

"Yes. The victim was definitely a male."

"The doctor is sure about that? The body was pretty dried up."

"There's no question about the sex. I saw the anatomical evidence myself, if you know what I mean."

"You don't have to protect my delicate sensibilities," Ortiz quipped. "After all, I was an AP the Air Force."

"Point noted," McKernan said with a smile.

"So what? The killer dressed the victim up as a woman before he dumped him in the tunnel?"

"No, it seems likely that the victim was dressed as he was at the time of the murder. There is evidence that he had undergone procedures to make him look more like a woman, procedures that aren't available on Mars. Also, the dye job to the hair had occurred long enough before death that the roots were starting to show."

"What do you mean by procedures?" Gaeretts asked.

"Some plastic surgery to the face, permanent removal of facial hair."

"Oh," the sergeant responded. "Not the other."

"No, not the other. Like I said, I saw the evidence."

"Who's the delicate one," Ortiz interjected. "You two are waltzing around the subject like a couple of old ladies. Why don't you just come out and say that the victim still had his balls?"

"So how did a guy like that get to Mars?" Gaeretts asked.

"That's a good question," McKernan replied. "Anyone with tendencies like the victim should have been weeded out by the mandatory psych screening everyone coming to Mars has to undergo. It's clear that the victim had exhibited the behavior before coming to Mars. Somehow, the screening process was subverted."

"So who was he?"

"The doctor wasn't able to ID the victim. The fingerprints are pretty degraded by the mummification. DNA should give us a positive ID, but the samples have to be sent back to Earth, so we won't have any help there for more than a month. There's nothing traceable about the clothing he was wearing which was limited to the dress and a pair of panties. No bra."

"Swell," Gaeretts exclaimed. "So where does that leave us?"

"The way I see it is we've got to find the answers to three questions," McKernan said. "First, who was the victim? Second, how did he get to Mars? Somehow he eluded the screening system. Either there is some sort of clandestine smuggling going on or he had the help of someone with enough pull to work the system. Either way, we've got a problem. But the third and most important question is, who is the killer?"

"No possibility that it was an accident?"

"Let's face it. The killer strangled the victim to the point of unconsciousness and stuffed him down into the utility tunnel in Corridor C. The intention was that he die."

"That's cold," Ortiz remarked.

"Yes, about five degrees above zero. No matter what shape the guy was in after the strangling, he probably never had a chance. It would only take a couple of hours for someone dressed as he was to die under those conditions. He wasn't meant to be found."

"You think the killer is still on Mars?" Ortiz asked.

"Maybe, maybe not. The doctor wasn't sure, but she thought the body could have been down in that tunnel for years. Maybe the killer has gone home to Earth. Or maybe he hasn't. One thing I know is that if he has killed once, he may kill again. I want to get him before he does."

"So what can we do?" Ortiz asked.

"We try to find answers to our questions, starting with the first one. You were looking for something to do. This is it. I want you to check all the databases. Ship manifests, payroll, anything you can think of. See if you can spot our victim. People don't just vanish on Mars. They've got to arrive on a spaceship, and go through the arrival procedure at the port. They have to eat and drink water. Somewhere in all that data there has got to be some clue as to who the victim was. You probably need to go back three years at least. Maybe even five."

"Ok," Ortiz said eagerly. "I'll get right on it."

"And while you're at it, you might see if any working girls have gone missing in that time frame."

"You think it wasn't just because he was a guy in a dress that he was killed?"

"It's a possibility we can't afford to overlook. My guess is that our victim was hanging out in one of the saloons that cater to miners and construction workers. Trying to cage a drink or a meal. Let's face it, with seven men to every woman, a lot of those guys aren't that particular, and if they're drunk, not even that perceptive. Maybe our killer picked up the victim and discovered that he wasn't a she and reacted. Or maybe he just likes to pick up women and beat them up. We need to find out."

"Sure thing."

"What do you want me to do, Chief?" Gaeretts asked.

"That utility guy, what was his name, Flint? He said that there were tunnels that no one had been in in years. We need to check them out."

"You think there are more bodies down there?"

"We won't know until we look. See if you can get the utilities to do an inspection. If not, you may have to do it yourself. But I want every tunnel, unused airlock, storage locker and any other place you can think of checked out."

"That's going to take a lot of time, Chief."

"You better get started, then. Use anyone that isn't busy. But don't use any overtime. Not yet. I still have a budget I have to meet."

"Gotcha. I'll see if I can get those dead heads in utilities to do the leg work."

"That's all I can think of, right now, but if either of you get any bright ideas, let me know."

Chapter 8: They Serve Takeout, Too

McKernan retired to the small cubicle that served as his office and spent much of the morning working on budget requests for the next fiscal year. As all funding for the department passed through the U.N Trust Authority, it was at the mercy of a small committee on Earth comprised solely of people who had never been to Mars, never would go to Mars, and who couldn't care less what happened on Mars. Their only concerns were the parochial politics of the nations in whose name they had been appointed, and their primary interest was in playing off one major power against another to maximize the benefits to their home countries. The only role Mars played was in supplying the mining concession fees and taxes that filled the coffers from which the U.N. largess was dispersed. Any expense on Mars was seen as a diminishment of that fund. For two budget cycles he had been trying to get through authorization for two more constables to patrol the vast areas outside Mars City and the major mining camps without success. He doubted that he would succeed with the new budget, either, but at least he would make the effort.

He was only too happy when his communicator alerted him of an incoming call, especially when he noted that the caller was Dr. Haestert.

"Hi, Beth. Do you have anything new for me?"

"Not much, I'm afraid, Inspector, but I do have a few things I'd like to show you if you have the time."

Seeing the time on the communicator screen he asked, "Have you had lunch yet?"

"No. Did you want to meet at the cafeteria?"

"I've got a better idea. When will you be free?"

"I take an hour break at noon."

"Good. I'll stop by the hospital and pick you up then."

"I'll be waiting," the doctor replied before hanging up.

Somehow, McKernan had lost interest in the budget requests. He spent the half hour until noon thinking about the doctor and wondering what she had for him.

It was no surprise, then, that the inspector arrived at the hospital promptly at noon. The doctor was in the lobby waiting for him. He noted that she was carrying a comp tablet.

"I thought that we could skip the cafeteria and try a little place that I know."

"That sounds interesting," Beth said, a little uncertainly. "I don't really get out much."

"It's not far, just a little ways down Corridor B."

"Hut Town?" she asked, raising her eyebrow.

"Don't look so concerned," McKernan reassured her. "Most of Hut Town is pretty civilized."

"I'm game," she responded, not completely convincingly.

He led her across the central corridor and down the tunnel to the lock for Corridor B.

"I take it you haven't been out to Hut Town much."

"Not much need to. So far most of my time has been spent between the hospital and the Women's Quarters."

"You're missing a lot," he said as he opened the lock hatch.

After they had passed through into the first section of Corridor B, the doctor gave a little shiver. "I didn't realize it would be so cold."

"We're no longer buried here, so no insulation. Heating takes energy, energy takes money. The Trust Authority doesn't spend any more money in Hut Town that it doesn't have to."

"So why would anyone live or work here?"

"Because it's cheap and because there's room. Lots of people would rather live out here than in a dormitory."

"You sound as if you approve."

"I'm one of them. I've got a place about a half kilometer down this corridor."

"You're proving to be full of surprises."

"You haven't seen anything, yet."

They continued to walk down the corridor, passing through a lock into the next section. They stopped before a hatch above which was a sign in Indian characters below which were the words "Hot Curry" in English.

"This is it," McKernan said.

"An Indian restaurant?" the doctor asked.

"Or a reasonable facsimile." He opened the hatch and they stepped inside. Immediately they were assaulted by a mélange of odors. After the cold of the corridor the small room seemed hot and humid as if they had been transported to the Indian subcontinent. The space of the hut, about the same size as McKernan's, had been divided in two by a counter. In the front part there were a few small mismatched tables, while behind the counter was the kitchen area from which emanated the sounds of Indian dance music. In addition to the tables there were a half dozen stools so patrons could eat at the counter.

A brown skinned woman behind the counter waved at them as they entered. "Hello, Inspector. Two for you and the lady?" she asked in precise but Mumbai-accented English.

"That would be perfect," McKernan responded. "We'll just grab a table."

"It will only be a few minutes then."

As they sat at a table in the corner McKernan said, "I'm sorry there's no menu. It's a case of whatever they have the ingredients for."

"This place is amazing," the doctor said, waving her hand around the room. The walls had been painted an almost violent yellow and been decorated enthusiastically if not expertly with the silhouettes in green of various tropical vegetation. "Why—, I mean how did someone end up doing this?"

"It's fairly typical, actually. Indira's husband came to Mars about five years ago as a geophysicist working for one of the mining companies. He came out on the usual three year contract. Halfway through, his brother was killed in a terrorist attack in Mumbai. He decided he didn't want to go back, so he brought his wife to Mars. She didn't really have the skills to get a job, so he took the bonus money he got for renewing his contract and they opened this place."

As he was explaining, the cook came out with two steaming plates of a curry rich with vegetables and two glasses of a curiously colored liquid.

The doctor took a tentative forkful of her food. Her eyes widened. "I wasn't expecting it to be so spicy."

"You've been eating at the cafeteria too much," McKernan said.

"Don't get me wrong. This is good. It's just that I wasn't expecting something so, well, flavorful. How does she do it?"

"They grow most of the peppers and things in a green house off the back of the hut. Some of the spices, too, though they do import some of those from Earth. The rest of the vegetables they get from local farms. About the only other thing from Earth is the rice and flour for the naan. When you think about it, Indian cuisine is a natural for Mars. Vegetables are easy to grow. Grains and meat consume a lot more resources and space."

"I'll have to remember this place."

"They serve takeout, too," McKernan said.

They both ate with relish for a few minutes. When they both were slowing down, McKernan asked, "So what have you got for me?"

"Not much, I'm afraid. The tox screen came back negative, but that may not mean much after the amount of time since death. There's no other evidence of drug use, though."

"Well, that's something. Any clue as to the identity?"

"I may have something for you there. I took the biometric data, height, weight, some other physical characteristics and compared them to the database. You know, of course, that all that information is kept on everyone who comes to Mars. Fortunately, the victim was outside the norms as far as size goes. He was a lot smaller than most males in the population. Most of the mining companies have minimum height and weight requirements, not surprising as they are mostly hiring miners and construction workers. At 165 centimeters, the victim is right at the low end cutoff. Same with his weight. Actually slightly below on that. Some of the U.N. staff tend to be smaller, though, depending on where they come from. I ignored age, as that could be faked on the records more easily than height or weight. When it comes down to it, there were only a limited number of possible matches in the database. Seven, in fact. Here's the list of names." She showed him the list on her tablet.

"Great. How many of these are still on Mars?"

"I'm afraid that I can't help you there. The records are added to the medical database when people arrive, but they often don't tell us when someone leaves. We'd only know if someone has died, or was treated and sent back to Earth for medical reasons."

"Still, it's something. I can have one of my people try to track down these seven so we may be able to identify our victim by elimination."

"There's one more thing I've got. I took the X-ray data and had the computer do a facial reconstruction. I'm no expert at that sort of thing, but this is what it came up with. I did it both with the hair as you found it and with it its natural color and more of a man's cut."

She turned the tablet so he could see the display. The images looked as if they could be brother and sister. He could see how the feminine version might be considered pretty in its own way. Somehow, the computer had managed to make both images look very sad.

Chapter 9: McKernan Talks to Power

After lunch McKernan walked the doctor back to the hospital and then returned to the police office. Ortiz was still there, busily working at a computer terminal behind the front desk.

"I've got some names for you to check out," he said as the constable looked up. "The doctor gave me a list of men that fit the basic physical parameters of the victim. I want you to track them down and see if any are missing. I've e-mailed you the list."

"That should make things easier," Ortiz said.

"Only if our victim is on that list. How are you doing so far?"

"It's slow going. The ship's passenger manifests are all on line, but after people land, things tend to be a lot more haphazard. I know where people were suppose to go according to the manifest, but there's no good way to verify that they actually went there. I can match names with people that return to Earth, but there's no tracking of them while they are here. Some of the mining companies have been helpful and anybody that works for the Trust Authority shows up, but some of the companies aren't cooperating, and independent contractors just fall through the cracks. And don't even talk to me about the Chinese. I can't get anything out of them."

"Well, fortunately our victim doesn't appear to be Asian. The doctor had the computer do a reconstruction of what our victim looked like before he got mummified."

He showed her the pictures.

"He wasn't bad looking, either as a man or a woman," Ortiz remarked.

"Yeah. Put out a notice on the newsfeed along with the picture asking anyone who recognizes him to contact us."

"Think anybody will reply?"

"It's worth a shot. But if he was hanging around the rough end of Hut Town, I wouldn't hold my breath. They tend to be pretty closed mouthed out there. Well, keep working and let me know if you come up with anything."

McKernan retired to his cubicle to work on budgets, but he found himself staring at the reconstructed faces instead. He hadn't got much done when his communicator buzzed angrily. He looked at the ID of the caller. It was George Entwhistle, the supervisor of the power plant. McKernan wondered what he wanted... or if he was calling to report that another body had been discovered.

"McKernan, that you? This is Entwhistle." The inspector reflected that some people still didn't get the idea of personal communicators and the fact that they displayed the identity of the caller.

"This is McKernan. What can I do for you?"

"You can get off my back, that's what," Entwhistle answered in an angry tone.

"I'm afraid I don't understand," McKernan responded softly.

"Your man Gaeretts was here. He wants me to search every inch of tunnel in Hut Town. Do you know how many men I've got working for me? Five, that's how many. Not including the two that I need to monitor the reactor. Do you have any idea how many kilometers of tunnel run under Hut Town?"

"No, I don't," answered McKernan. "That was why I had Sergeant Gaeretts contact you."

"Well I'll tell you how many kilometers. Over a hundred and twenty. And those are only the active ones with live feeds running through them. That doesn't count abandoned tunnels and stubs. I've got the blue prints right here to prove it."

"That's why I need your help, George. I don't know if you heard, but one of your men discovered a body in the tunnel under Corridor C yesterday."

"Yeah. Flint. He told me about it. Some working girl or something."

"Well, then he probably told you that the body had been there for a long time. Maybe years. What I'm worried about is that there might be more bodies out there in some little visited tunnel. That's why I need your help."

"Geez, McKernan. What are you talking about? Like a serial killer? On Mars? How can that happen? I mean isn't everyone supposed to be vetted by the Trust Authority?"

"That's the theory. But we haven't been able to identify the victim yet. Somehow, he went missing, and no one noticed or bothered to tell anyone. Obviously there are lapses in the system. Without knowing who the victim is we can't be sure what happened. That's why this is so important."

"I can see that. But what am I supposed to do? I don't have enough manpower to spare on a search that big."

"I understand, George. I don't expect your department to deal with this alone. I'll talk to the heads of water and air to get their help, too. And I can assign some of my people as well, maybe even get some volunteers. But I need someone who understands those tunnels to coordinate things. That's why I had Gaeretts contact you."

"Well he wasn't very clear about that."

"I apologize for that. The sergeant is sometimes lacking in tact."

"Yeah, well, I might have been a little gruff with him," Entwhistle replied, his tone moderating.

"I'm not asking for miracles, but we need to get this search done as soon as can be managed with the resources that we have available. It needs to be done efficiently, which is why you can be so helpful. You've got access to all the maintenance records and understand the system. If you take charge we won't be running around wasting time and chasing our tails." It never hurt to appeal to an engineer's vanity, McKernan thought to himself.

"I'll be glad to do my part, Erik. But it's going to take some time, even with all the other departments chipping in."

"I realize that, George. But the sooner we get started, the sooner we get the job done. And George, it's not just Hut Town. There's nothing to say that our killer, if there is one, didn't operate in Mars City itself."

"Here in Mars City? You're serious about that?"

"I'm afraid so, until we can rule it out. And it's not just the tunnels. He might have stuffed a body in any out of the way place. Unused airlocks, storage lockers, equipment bays. Well you've got a better idea of those things than I do."

"Geez McKernan. That's a lot of territory."

"I know, George. That's why I'm counting on you. And George, we don't want to start a panic over this. We need to be discrete."

"I understand, Erik."

"Thanks, George. Let me know if you need any support from my end with the other departments."

McKernan hung up his communicator. He wondered if he was making a mistake. So far all he had was a single body. There was no evidence that it was a serial killing. But he also knew that once a man kills, the likelihood of him killing again goes up.

He went back to the budget requests. Before he realized it, it was 1700 and Ortiz was knocking on his door.

"Chief, I'm going to knock off for the day. Ferris is here to man the desk."

"Good. I appreciate your pitching in, Ortiz. We're going to be busy until this thing is resolved. But don't overwork yourself. If you get tired or anything, let me know. We don't want any problems with the baby."

"I'll be fine, Chief."

"Good."

"Chief?" Ortiz asked tentatively.

"Yes?"

"I don't know if it means anything yet, but I've been tracking down the working girls in Hut Town. So far there are about a dozen that I can't account for."

"A dozen?" McKernan responded in surprise. "What do you mean you can't account for them?"

"They're in the records as arriving on Mars. They registered as prostitutes. But they haven't showed up for the mandatory monthly health check for a while and there's no record of them having returned to Earth. Maybe they've taken up other work, but I can't locate them."

"Any chance they've just gone freelance or are off the grid for some reason?"

"Sure. It's possible. I just started looking. But I thought you'd want to know."

"You're right. Thanks for telling me. I want you to keep checking on them. In the morning. Now get some dinner and a good night's rest. Good-night, Constable."

"Good-night, Inspector," Ortiz said as she close his office door.

After she left, McKernan sat there for a moment. A dozen women unaccounted for. And no one had a clue. He decided it was time to pay a visit to the wilder side of Hut Town.

Chapter 10: The Inspector Visits a Bordello

McKernan unlocked a drawer in his desk and withdrew a small bundle. This contained a shoulder holster and a small, 7 mm automatic pistol. He strapped the holster on, checked the pistol, verified that the safety was on, and replaced the weapon in its sheath. These days he didn't normally carry a firearm unless he was expecting trouble or planning on visiting the rougher parts of Hut Town. Guns were dangerous, particularly so in a pressurized environment where only a few centimeters of foam and a thin skin of aluminum stood between you and the near vacuum that was the atmosphere of Mars. To the inspector's mind, they were a weapon of last resort, more useful for their deterrent value than as something to be used.

He hadn't always been so casual. A few years back he had never gone anywhere unarmed, but Mars was changing, hopefully for the better. He checked the knife tucked into his boot top and the one in the sheath at his belt. Things might be more peaceful these days, but McKernan had learned from experience to be prepared. He pulled on a jacket, partly to conceal the pistol, but also because it would be cold where he was going.

The position of prostitution was a delicate one on Mars. In the early days when Mars had been a small scientific outpost with less than a thousand residents there had been no such thing. Everyone who made it to the planet had been a thoroughly vetted, dedicated individual. Stints on the planet were usually short, less than a year plus transit time. Also, the ratio between men and women had been, if not equal, at least close enough to avoid tension.

That had all changed when the planet had been opened up to mining. The insatiable demand of Earth for the so called rare earths, the elements vital to the superconductors, magnets, and solar cells necessary to meeting the planet's energy needs had served as the rationale for the development of Mars. The population soared tenfold in a matter of a few years. As most of the influx consisted of miners and construction workers, the sex ratio had skewed dramatically, reaching thirteen to one at its peak. Driven by cost considerations, the three year contract had become the standard. With no realistic outlet for the satisfying of sexual needs, the situation had become extremely volatile and Mars had become a dangerous place.

The mining companies had argued, probably correctly, that with so many men there was a need for what they termed "entertainment workers" to defuse the pent up needs of their workers. The Trust Authority had, of course, resisted, but money had won out. With a substantial portion of the licensing and extraction fees being split amongst the developing countries, there were only too many votes in the U.N. General Assembly interested in the smooth operation of the mines. The more "civilized" nations lost out. A compromise was reached.

The Trust Authority would allow a set number of "recreational staff" on the planet. These were to be considered as independent contractors, rather than employees of any corporation. Each recreational contractor was required to have a non-cancelable round trip ticket, would be required to register, and would need to submit to monthly health inspections to avoid STDs. Pimps and panderers were specifically barred, and anyone engaging in those activities could be immediately deported back to Earth. That, in theory, was the compromise.

As with any other business, economic considerations came into play, and while a small number of “working girls”, the current preferred euphemism on Mars, frequented the lounges of the Mars Hotel and the Mars Sheraton, the preponderance of the sex trade took place in the remote corners of Hut Town where rents were cheap and oversight minimal. This was where McKernan was headed.

The specific destination he had in mind was at the far limits of Corridor C. On Mars, as anywhere, location was everything in real estate. The most desirable properties in Hut Town were at the near end of the corridors close in towards Mars City proper. This was where the more respectable businesses were located, the merchants, outfitters, engineering firms and other legitimate operations. The residential section was a little farther out where cost mattered more than convenience. It was only out past the two kilometer mark, where expenses were nil, that the bars, flop huts, and honky-tonks that catered to miners in town for a few days of recreation or prospectors on a spree were located.

McKernan found himself retracing his steps past the point where the body had been discovered. He had been down the length of Corridor C hundreds of times, just as he had been down the other corridors radiating from the walls of Mars City. But he knew from experience that there was little to distinguish one section of corridor from another. In the dim light it would be easy to find oneself lost unless you paid attention to the lock numbers as you passed through them.

The far end of Corridor C had originally been the maintenance bays and warehouse space of the early settlement. Many of the huts were larger than the standard units which comprised most of Hut Town, making them desirable spaces for saloons and similar businesses. The fact that they were as far as possible from Mars City was an asset both ends appreciated.

As he stepped through the last of the locks, McKernan was hit by a blast of sound and the smell of unwashed bodies. Unlike the practice in the rest of Hut Town, the hatches on either side of the corridor were kept open, and the blare of music of sorts poured out from the interiors. The hatches were highlighted by garish signs detailing the attractions within. Reflexively his eyes looked through the hatch of "Thelma's", the largest and most raucous of the saloons, but it seemed relatively peaceful, probably because there were relatively few miners in town at the moment.

His goal was a few doors down, an establishment that proclaimed itself to be "Singapore Sam's" in mock Chinese lettering. The outdated Burmese rock playing inside brought back memories of his time as a pilot before he came to Mars. He pushed his way through the beaded curtain that shielded the hatchway into the dimly lit bar area within. A few bored looking women and one lone miner stood at one end of the bar. At the back of the room a short hallway receded into the gloom, punctuated by doors on either side every few meters.

A vaguely Asian man was manning the bar. "Hello, Inspector. No trouble here. Singapore Sam follow rules always."

"I haven't said you weren't," McKernan responded.

"Then why you here? You looking for girl. I can set you up with blonde, red-head, you name it."

"I'm not looking for a girl. And you know pimping is illegal."

"Sam not a pimp. I just charge small referral fee. All legal. .Make money by renting out rooms by hour. Much better. Everybody happy. Everything legal. So what you want? I got number one whiskey."

"I'll pass on the rot gut, Sam. What I want is some information."

"Information. Sure, Inspector. Anything you want to know. Sam happy to help police."

"Good. You heard about the body that was found?"

"Yeah. I watch newsfeed. I also hear that body was boy not woman. That true?"

"Yeah. That's true. You didn't recognize the picture, did you?"

"Singapore Sam's not that kind of place. Only number one girls work here. All real women. Sam knows. I check. No complaints."

"Yeah. I can see that. The thing is, in checking up, we've discovered a number of working girls have gone missing. You know anything about that?"

"Missing? What you mean?"

"They've stopped showing up for their health inspections and they haven't gone back to Earth. I want to know what's happened to them."

"You know, Inspector, girls come and go all a time. Go work someplace else. Maybe come back, maybe not. They independent contractors. U.N. say so. Not my job to keep track."

"I know. It's not your job. But what happened to them?"

"It's like this, Inspector," Sam said, suddenly dropping his accent. "Sometimes the girls get tired of working. Some prospector or someone else takes a shine to a particular woman. Asks her to go out prospecting or whatever. Ain't one of these girls doesn't get propositioned at least once a month. Sometimes they take him up on it. Sometimes they come back after a couple of months of living in a tin can, sometimes they don't. It's impossible to keep track. Maybe the prospector gets tired of the woman after a couple of months and she ends up in the desert, not that I've never heard of that actually happening."

"So you never heard of a woman just going missing?"

"Hard to say. Sometimes it's a spur of the moment kind of thing. Too much booze. Gone in the morning. Most of the working girls travel pretty light. They don't keep a lot of stuff. Just what they can pack in a bag. Some of them change flops pretty frequently. Most of my girls now, they're pretty regular. I treat them right."

"Yeah, I'm sure, Sam."

"You insult me, inspector.

"So you don't know anything?" McKernan asked.

"You serious about girls maybe getting killed and dumped in the tunnels?"

"Maybe. I don't know. That's why I'm asking."

"Look. I'd tell you if I knew of anything. But I don't. I'll keep my ears open. I'll talk to the girls, too, fat lot of good that will do. None of them listen to me. Sure you don't want some whiskey? It almost tastes like the real thing."

"Thanks, Sam. But no thanks."

With that McKernan left. He tried a few other places, but kept getting the same answers. After a while, he gave it up and headed home.

CHAPTER 11: FIVE FOUND ALIVE, TWO DEAD

It was late, after 10:00, when McKernan got into the office. Gaeretts was manning the front desk, while Ortiz was seated at a computer screen in the back of the room. Both gave their boss a questioning look when he walked in but neither said a word.

"Anything happen overnight that I should know about?" McKernan asked.

"Pretty quiet night, Chief. A couple of drunk miners. Ferris put them to bed without any trouble. How was Singapore Sam's?" Gaeretts asked with a leer.

"Pretty useless," the inspector replied ignoring the innuendo. "According to Sam, working girls come and working girls go, and no one seems to keep track. I got the feeling half the prostitutes in Hut Town could disappear and no one would think of mentioning it."

"Yeah, they tend to keep their mouths shut out at the ends of the corridors," Gaeretts grunted.

"How's the search of the tunnels going?"

"I talked to Entwhistle this morning. He's working on a search plan. He figures it will take about a week to make a pass through all the tunnels using personnel from the various utilities departments. That's just walking the tunnels. It doesn't include poking noses into all the dark corners."

"Well, have him go ahead. And tell him to have his men keep an eye out for any footprints that don't belong. The dust is so thick in some of those tunnels that anybody that's been through there in the last couple of years would leave a trail."

"We've already discussed that. His men are supposed to note any signs of 'unusual' activity so we can follow up on it. Personally, I think that if another corpse is going to be found, they're hoping it's one of us rather than one of them."

"Can you blame them?" McKernan said, passing through the counter to the back of the room.

"Anything new on your end, Ortiz?" McKernan asked as he walked past her desk.

"I've tracked down those seven names you gave me, Inspector."

McKernan had noticed that Ortiz tended to use his title when she was making an official report. Probably because of her training in the Air Police. He reflected that there were worse habits.

"And?"

"Three of them are still on Mars. I talked to them over their communicators and verified their status. Two of the seven have returned to Earth. I sent packet messages to both of them. Just got the last reply."

Because of the distance between Earth and Mars it took anywhere from eight minutes to an hour for radio or light to make the trip there and back there was no such thing as a normal conversation. The standard procedure was to record a packet of voice or video, compress it and send it as one short burst using a tight beam laser. One tried to get as much into each burst so as to cut down the number of packets going back and forth. Communication between the planets wasn't particularly expensive, it was just clumsy.

"I take it both of them are still alive?"

"That's right, Inspector."

"That leaves two," McKernan said, pointing out the obvious.

"Both are dead. Killed on Mars in accidents."

Not surprising, McKernan thought. Mars had plenty of ways to kill a man. Accidents were the leading cause of death.

"You followed up to make sure?"

"Yeah. One of them, Julio Fujiwara was a geological technician working out at Anglo-Martian #3. He was killed in a freak accident. A Mars buggy passing by kicked up a chunk of rock that hit him square in the faceplate of his helmet while he was outside taking samples. Shattered the plastic. He died before they could get him into a pressurized area. The guy I talked to out there had been standing right next to him when it happen. I could tell that he was still pretty shaken up about the whole thing. He's definitely not our corpse."

"And the other one?"

"Mario Guzman. He was working at one of the camps of Rio Plata Mining. He was killed in an accident a little over two years ago." Rio Plata was a relative newcomer to Mars, a third world company that had gotten a mining concession for political reasons. McKernan didn't know much about them.

"The report said he had a suit malfunction. He'd only been on Mars three months." The first six months on Mars were the most dangerous. That was the period before taking precautions and double checking every detail became a force of habit.

"You sound like you're not convinced," McKernan said, noting the tone of suspicion in the constable's voice.

"The report is all in order. The camp doctor and manager both signed off on it. There's just one thing—"

"Which is?" McKernan asked, wondering if Ortiz was on to something or just being overly dramatic.

"The body was sent back to Earth."

"You're sure about that?" Considering the cost of freight, that was highly unusual. There was a clause in the standard work contract that specifically stated that in the case of death there would be no repatriation of the remains.

"I've got a copy of the shipping manifest right here. I asked around. It turns out Guzman was related to one of the big wigs of Rio Plata. I don't know what a kid like that was doing on Mars."

"So they sent the body back to Earth. Any chance we can verify the remains?" He wasn't looking forward to trying to have a body exhumed on Earth, but maybe he'd get lucky and some local coroner on Earth had done an autopsy or something.

"That's just it, sir. The body was cremated."

"You're sure of that?"

"Yes, sir. I've got copies of the death certificate and cremation papers. They're in Spanish, but I'm good enough in the language to read them."

"Why would they go to the expense of shipping the body back to Earth and then cremate it when they could have cremated it on Mars and save themselves the cost of shipping back sixty or seventy extra kilos?"

"That's what I was thinking, sir. It doesn't make sense."

"I guess rich people just don't think about things like money."

"There's one other thing, sir," Ortiz said.

"You're enjoying this aren't you, Ortiz? Well, what is it?"

"I've got a picture of Guzman. Compare it to the reconstruction Dr. Haestert did." The constable brought up both pictures side by side on her screen.

McKernan looked at the two. Within the limitations of the reconstruction, the two images could easily be of the same person.

"Can you bring up images of the other six names on the list?" McKernan asked.

"Sure. Give me a second."

One by one Ortiz brought up the images None was a particularly close match, certainly not as close as Guzman.

"OK, Ortiz. You've made your point. Guzman could be our victim. Except for the fact that he died out at a mining camp. And the fact that the body was sent back to Earth. How do you explain that?"

"I can't, Inspector."

"Neither can I, Ortiz. I want you to see what you can dig up about Guzman's demise and subsequent travels. See if you can find anything, autopsy, custom's inspection, anything that would indicate that there really was a body that was shipped back to Earth to be burned up."

"I'll get right on it sir." Ortiz replied promptly.

"And Ortiz, good work."

McKernan went on into his office. He noted that Ortiz had passed on the files on Guzman to his computer. Pulling the two images up on his screen, he found himself staring at the two faces that looked so much alike.

It didn't make sense. If Guzman was the body that had been found in the tunnel, why go to all the trouble of faking his death and sending something that weighed seventy or eighty kilos by the time you included the coffin or body bag or whatever had been used to package the corpse, at a hundred or two hundred dollars a kilo? What could they be trying to hide?

Chapter 12: A Second Opinion

McKernan kept staring at the two images throughout the morning. The resemblance might be accidental, but it kept bugging him. Finally, just before noon, he decided to take action. What he needed was a second opinion, someone with a trained eye. Grabbing his computer pad he headed for the hospital.

He asked the nurse on duty if Dr. Haestert was in. She just pointed to the back. McKernan thought he detected the hint of a smile on her face.

"Erik. What brings you here? " the doctor asked. She seemed pleased to see him. "Are you asking me out to lunch again, or is this a professional visit?"

"The latter, I'm afraid. I'm here for a second opinion."

"Is this related to the body?" she asked, sounding disappointed.

"I had Ortiz, one of my constables, track down the names on the list you gave me. She found three of them still alive on Mars and two who had gone back to Earth. The other two died on Mars of accidents."

"Is that Elena Ortiz?" she asked.

"Yes, why?"

"Just curiosity. I'm acting as her ob/gyn, that's all."

"Oh. I hope everything is going all right. She said that you had ordered her to stay in Mars City until after the birth."

"She's doing fine. It's just a precaution. There haven't been that many babies born on Mars, so each one is still a new experience. Actually, Elena is healthy as a horse. From what I can tell, she eats better than most people on Mars."

"Good. I'd hate for anything to go wrong."

"You like her, don't you?" the doctor asked.

"She's a good cop. Smart, good people skills, tough when she has to be. I'd hate to lose her."

"So what are you going to do after the baby is born?"

"I guess I haven't thought about it."

"It's time you do. The baby is due in only eight weeks."

"She'll get time off, of course. Technically, she's on paid leave now. She's only been doing work in the office because she was bored. Once she's ready to come back to duty, she's got a man and friends out at Junction 3 that can take care of the kid when she's out on patrol.

"Assuming she wants to go back to duty," the doctor remarked.

"I think she will. Being a cop has gotten into her blood."

"We'll see," the doctor replied. Changing the subject she said, "I guess that list was a dead end. You said you had accounted for all of the names I gave you."

"Yeah, we tracked down the five that are still alive and have got the death reports on the two that aren't. But there's something strange about one of them. That's why I came to see you. I want you to take a look at this picture of one of the dead men, Mario Guzman."

He brought up the image on his pad. He could tell by the doctor's expression that the resemblance had struck her as well.

"Of course, it could be a coincidence. Same physical size, ethnic background, age. And of course the reconstruction isn't perfect. I'm far from an expert in that area. But it sure looks like the same man to me. You're sure he died as reported?"

"That's just it. The accident occurred out at one of the mining camps. The report said suit failure, which could mean almost anything. But the body was sent back to Earth and then cremated."

"Cremated? On Earth? That's pretty unusual, isn't it?"

"I've never heard of it happening before, not in that order. A few bodies have been cremated here on Mars and the remains sent back to Earth, but not sent back before cremation. It just doesn't make sense financially. We're talking tens of thousands of dollars more."

"That's what I thought."

"Yeah, so there's no way to verify that there even was a body. All I have to go on at this point is the paperwork."

"Is there some other explanation for the resemblance? Did the this Guzman have a sibling or a cousin on Mars."

"Not that I know of, but Ortiz is trying to find out more about him. Maybe something will show up. But if he did have a twin or a cousin or something that was about the same size, why didn't he show up on your list?"

"Good point. He should have if he was here officially."

"It's starting to look like I have an even bigger mystery on my hands," McKernan said. "By the way, you mentioned lunch. Does that mean you're interested?"

"I'm afraid I'll have to take a rain check," the doctor replied. "We're expecting a casualty to be coming in any minute. A construction worker broke his arm and suffered some exposure from a tear in his suit. Fortunately, they got a patch on the suit in time, but there still was significant trauma. Some other time, though—"

"I'll keep that in mind," McKernan said with a smile. "I'd better clear out of here then—"

In place of lunch with the doctor McKernan grabbed a soy dog from the food cart on the main concourse and headed back to the office.

"So what did the doctor think?" Ortiz asked.

"She thought it was a remarkable resemblance. While you're checking up on Guzman's corpse, why don't you see if he has any close relatives about the same age and see if any of them happen to have been on Mars in the last few years. And anything else useful that you can think of, too."

McKernan retired to his cubicle to eat his soy dog, though the idea appealed to him even less than it did before.

Chapter 13: Dinner With the Doctor

McKernan spent an unsatisfactory afternoon working on budgets for the next biennium, a period that conveniently almost coincided with the length of the Martian year. Not for the first time he wondered when the people living on Mars would order their lives around the cycles of that planet rather than those of a planet that seemed more remote and artificial with each passing year. Would it happen when they received some degree of local self-government, or would it have to wait until some distant day when either the planet or its residents had changed enough so that they could actually go outside and feel the changing of the seasons? No matter which, the budgets he was working on would be sent to the Trust Authority on Earth for review and changed, invariably downward, by a committee composed of bureaucrats who had never and would never set foot on Mars.

He was about to pack it in and head home for a lonely and uninspiring dinner when his communicator buzzed with an incoming call. It was from Dr. Haestert.

"Hi, Beth," McKernan said as he answered the call.

"Hi, Erik. Have I hit you at a convenient time?"

"Perfect. I was just about to head home. How's your emergency?"

"He's fine. Fine that is, except for a compound fracture of his forearm and a touch of frostbite where his suit was punctured. He should recover nicely."

"Glad to hear it," McKernan responded.

"Look, I'm sorry about lunch, but are you free for dinner? I've got a few things I'd like to discuss with you about Guzman."

"Sure, sounds good. Where do you want to eat?"

"As you seem to be the local authority on dining, why don't you choose?"

"OK. Are you free now?"

"My shift ends in about fifteen minutes."

"I'll stop by the hospital then."

"I'll be waiting," the doctor said, a note of anticipation in her voice.

With a few minutes to kill, McKernan wandered out into the police station's bullpen. Ortiz was still there, busy at a computer.

"Anything new?"

"I'm still waiting for a response from the authorities in Montevideo. That's where the remains were sent. I haven't a clue as to what the local time is there, so we probably won't hear back until tomorrow at the earliest. I did get a copy of Guzman's personnel file from Rio Plata. It makes for some interesting reading. Also makes you wonder what this guy was doing on Mars in the first place. He had no degree, no useful skills, nothing to qualify him for a job at a mining camp. Bright enough guy, though. He was studying art at a university in Argentina, but never finished, just left in the middle of a term."

"That is curious. What was his job description at Rio Plata?"

"Rigger!" She answered with astonishment.

McKernan could understand the constable's amazement. "Rigger" was a term used for general labor involved in setting up mining and construction equipment. The usual type was long on brawn and short on brains or as short as you could be and still pass the competitive selection process for employment on Mars. From his file, Guzman would appear singularly unsuited for that type of work.

"How long was he there before the accident that killed him?"

"The file says just under six months. Which is about all it says," Ortiz said with a touch of sarcasm. "There are no details about work assignments, what crew he was on, performance evaluations. None of the usual stuff that you would expect. He showed up on Mars, drew his pay, which coincidentally was about twice the usual wage for a rigger, and then bam we have the accident and the body is shipped back to Earth on a company ship."

The latter was unusual. A few of the mining companies maintained their own ships, but most used the regular liners run by Interplanetary Transport. Those that did operate their own ships were mostly Chinese or Russian. Spaceships were expensive to own and operate.

"This is starting to sound interesting. Keep at it and keep me up to date on what you find. But don't work too long. Seems you're spending all you time here at the station."

"It's less lonely than the women's quarters. I'm starting to miss Junction 3. It's not much, but at least I know everyone there."

"OK. Just don't work too hard. And get something to eat."

"Gaeretts is going to bring in dinner. What about you?"

"I've got a date for dinner."

"The doctor?" Ortiz smirked.

"Yes, if you must know. She wants to discuss the case," McKernan said defensively.

"Have a nice time, sir."

The doctor was waiting in the hospital lobby when he arrived.

"Sorry if I kept you waiting," McKernan said.

"No, I just checked out a moment ago. So, where are we going? Another place in Hut Town?" She was beginning to say it as one word like the natives.

"Let it be a surprise."

This time they headed out Corridor A. A short walk down the corridor just past the second lock brought them to a hatch above which was a bold sign in pink letters.

"The Pork Palace?" the doctor queried.

"Hey, pigs are the perfect source of protein for Mars. They don't require a lot of space and they'll eat anything. All of the pigs served here are raised locally and butchered in the back of the restaurant."

"Sounds yummy," Beth said skeptically.

"Well, it is eclectic. If it can be made with a pig they'll try to make it. Not always successfully, but at least it's never boring. Shall we?"

"Lead on."

McKernan opened the hatch and they stepped through. The dining room was at least ten degrees warmer than the corridor and filled with the odors of frying pork, onions and peppers. Seating consisted of booths separated by thin plastic panels. A small light fixture suspended from the ceiling hung above each of the tables. A discerning eye would have recognized them as repurposed emergency lights used in mining tunnels. Despite the utilitarian nature of the décor, the results were surprisingly intimate.

They grabbed an open booth. Moments later, a waiter appeared from the kitchen carrying a plastic slate with the days menu written on it in erasable marker.

"Beer? Wine? Water?" he asked.

"Beer for me," McKernan said.

"How's the wine?" the doctor asked.

"Red. Or White. Whichever you prefer," the waiter answered. "Personally, I'd stick to the beer."

"Alright. Beer, then."

"I'll bring your drinks, and be back to take your order," the waiter said before disappearing into the kitchen.

They looked over the menu, sharing the slate between them.

"Any recommendations?"

"The schnitzel is usually good. Or the pork, vegetables and fried rice. I'd stay away from the cabbage rolls, but that's a personal preference."

"What are you having?"

"I think I'll try the sausage and fried potatoes."

The doctor settled on the schnitzel which was served with peppers and onions with fried potatoes on the side. The beers arrived, an amber liquid served in liter sized plastic mugs.

"This tastes nothing like the beer in the commissary," the doctor remarked after taking a tentative sip.

"You mean it tastes like something," McKernan responded. "You said you had something to discuss?"

"Only that I had a chance to look over Guzman's medical file while I was waiting for our emergency."

"And?"

"The file doesn't really add up. It's almost as if someone had just filled in the blanks without knowing anything about the patient. There's the usual, height, weight, etc. but the psych eval just reads like cookie cutter verbiage if you know what I mean."

"Like someone was trying to cover something up?"

"Maybe. Or was just told to fill it out to make it look good. Well, not good, just unremarkable. No phobias, no neurosis, no traumatic incidents. But it also says that Guzman's mother died at an early age. There should have been at least a little follow up on that. And what was he doing on Mars? I've seen enough patients here to know he wasn't your typical miner."

"Ortiz and I were just talking about the same thing. He was ten centimeters too short and twenty kilos too light for a job as a rigger. I've known some pretty strong short guys, but from his file Guzman didn't strike me as having that type of physique."

"That's what I thought," the doctor continued. "Another thing is the medical report after the accident that killed him."

"Oh?" McKernan responded.

"It just doesn't read like a real report. I don't know the doctor who filled it out, he was employed by the mining company and returned to Earth before I got here, but his report seems more like a work of fiction than a real report."

"What exactly do you mean?"

"It's just too pat. Too dispassionate. No real details. It reads like a training scenario or test question. Just out of curiosity, I looked up some other accident reports filed by the same doctor. They read like I'd expect an accident report to. Guzman's report just doesn't match the others."

"So your saying that death report was faked?"

"I'm saying I don't think the doctor ever saw the body."

They sat in silence for a moment drinking their beers. Then the doctor asked, "What do you think about your victim?"

"What do you mean?"

"Well, it's apparent that he had some gender identity issues. What are your feelings about people like that?"

McKernan was thoughtful for a moment. "I decided a long time ago that it wasn't by business to judge people's lifestyles as long as they didn't cause problems. In my line of work it makes things easier. I can't say that I'd be comfortable with a guy like that, but I wouldn't get upset."

"But do you think people like that should be on Mars?"

"That's not my call, fortunately. But Mars is a rough place. A guy like that was bound to run into problems. But no one deserves to die like he did, freezing and unconscious in the bottom of a tunnel. What do you think?"

"I don't know. The psychology of sexual orientation isn't my field of expertise. I guess I've never really had to think about it before. And as you say, Mars is a rough place. But it makes me sad. Why didn't he stay home? There are plenty of places on Earth where he would have been accepted."

"That's the question. What was he doing on Mars? He certainly didn't belong here."

McKernan stared into his beer. They were saved from further discussion on the subject by the arrival of their dinners.

Chapter 14: Ortiz Hits a Wall

When McKernan arrived at the police station the next morning, Ortiz, as was becoming a habit, was already there. She eyed her boss speculatively, wondering just how dinner with the doctor had gone. The chief inspector's face revealed no clue.

"Any new developments?" he asked passing through to his own office.

"Nothing new from Earth. It's almost as if they're ignoring me while trying to appear to be helpful. I keep getting copies of the same Customs and cremation burial forms from the authorities in Uruguay, but nothing more. I know my Spanish isn't so bad that they could misunderstand me, but just to make sure I sent the same requests for information in English."

"Well, it's not like a request for information on the disposition of the body of a two year old accident victim would be a priority—" McKernan commented.

"Maybe not, but I asked specifically if there had been any local autopsy or examination of the body by Customs. They won't even say yes or no. Just no answer. I'm getting frustrated."

"Give them a few more days. If we don't get any help I can try to get the Trust Authority to put some pressure on them."

"I did find out some other information, though," Ortiz said.

"Well?" McKernan asked somewhat impatiently.

"You asked me to see if Mario Guzman had any siblings or cousins. There wasn't anything in his personnel file, but I did some poking around press archives in Montevideo. He was an only child, and none of his cousins were close to the same age, but I did find out who his father was."

"Are you going to keep me guessing?"

"It turns out his father was and still is the Vice President for Interplanetary Operations for the Rio Plata Mining Company. His grandfather is the chairman. Between the various branches, the Guzman family owns over half of the stock in the company."

"That explains why they might want to ship Mario's body back to Earth and why they could afford to. It still doesn't explain what he was doing on Mars in the first place."

"I don't know. Maybe he was sent out to Mars to get some real world experience so that he would be ready to take over from his father at some point. Rich families do that kind of thing, don't they?"

"You're asking me?" McKernan said with a laugh. "I might buy that if he had been working as a clerk or accountant or something. But a rigger? That's dangerous work for which the boy would have been completely unsuited."

"Maybe they had someone baby-sitting him so he wouldn't get into trouble," Ortiz suggested.

"If they did, he wasn't very good at his job. There's got to be some other reason why he was on Mars. I think I'd like to know some more about the Family Guzman. Like, if Mario was an only child, what would happen to his father's share of the business if he should die?"

"You think that maybe Mario's death wasn't an accident?" Ortiz asked, her eyes suddenly wide.

"I don't know. But a lot of people seem to have gone to great lengths to not make information available. The doctor seems to think that his medical records were fabricated at least in part. That includes the accident report. At the least it's suspicious." He gave her a quick précis of his conversation with Dr. Haestert at dinner.

"The doctor seems to have come to the same conclusions we have," Ortiz commented when he had finished.

"And Ortiz, try to keep you investigation discrete. We don't need to tick off one of the mining companies, particularly if all they're trying to do is keep family matters private. And remember, we still have a murder to solve. We still don't have any evidence that the body that was found in the tunnel was Mario Guzman. The two may be totally unrelated."

"Do you really think that, Inspector?"

"No. But until we have solid proof we at least have to act that way." He turned and went into his office.

A few hours later there was a discrete knock on the partition wall of his office. It was Ortiz.

"I looked into the Guzmans and Rio Plata. It seems that the stock is held in some sort of complicated family trust or something. I'm not enough of a lawyer to understand all the details. Anyway, the stock is apportioned amongst the old man and his various children. He has five. They can pass the stock onto their descendents, but if any of the family members should die without survivors, their stock reverts back to the trust."

"In other words, with Mario dead, if his father dies, his shares would be split up amongst his brothers and sisters," McKernan said.

"That's right. And the total value of the Guzmans' stake in Rio Plata is roughly twelve billion."

"Dollars?" McKernan asked.

"Yes, but with those kind of numbers does it matter? I couldn't find out exactly what Mario's father's share is, but it has to be at least two billion if the shares are divided equally. That's a lot of money. Enough to be a reason to knock off a cousin or nephew."

"Were there any family members on Mars at the time of Mario's death?"

"I'm trying to find that out now. Do you really think a family member would commit murder in person?"

"Would you trust an outsider? Who knows. This might just be a case of greed, or it might be part of some feud between different branches of the family. Keep this under your hat, Ortiz. If word gets out that the owners of one of the major mining companies are being investigated for murder there will be hell to pay. Don't even talk about it to Gaeretts until we know more one way or the other."

Chapter 15: A Second Corpse

At 16:00 McKernan was debating whether he should call Beth to see if she wanted to go to dinner again when Gaeretts popped into his office.

"Chief, I just got a call from Entwhistle. One of his men has found another body."

"Where?"

"The farthest out cross tunnel between Corridor B and C. It was hidden in some kind of equipment cabinet or something."

"Grab the crime scene kit," the inspector said rising from his desk. On his way out he called to Ortiz, "Man the front desk until Gaeretts gets back."

"Yes, sir," the constable replied as he cycled through the hatch, not waiting for Gaeretts.

Once outside in the corridor, McKernan slowed after the first rush of adrenalin. If it was a body, and he had no reason to doubt it was, there really was no point in hurrying. If it was like the last, it might have been there for years.

By the time he had reached the main concourse, Gaeretts had caught up with him, the older man puffing noticeably.

"Corridor B or C?" he asked.

"C's closer, probably quicker," McKernan replied. "Not that it really matters."

The two policemen walked rapidly down the hallway leading to C Corridor in silence. There was really no point in speculation until they reached the scene.

Unlike the corridors, the cross tunnels were not penetrated by the hatches of huts. They had been built originally only as convenient short cuts between the corridors back when all of Mars City had been housed in huts. Corridors B and C ran parallel to each other roughly a hundred and twenty meters apart, with a cross linking tunnel every couple of hundred meters until near the corridor's far end.

Unlike the corridors, which were level, the cross tunnels sloped down from each end so that at the midpoint the top of the tunnel was below grade. This had been done so that surface vehicles could drive over the tunnels if need be. The tunnels were also made from a smaller tube, only a little over three meters in diameter. With the cables and plumbing that ran along the sides of the tunnel, there was only about a meter of clear walk way running down the center. The only locks were at each end where they intersected with the corridors though there were several emergency hatches exiting to the surface.

It was noticeably colder when McKernan and Gaeretts stepped through the lock into the tunnel. McKernan wished he had brought gloves. The only light was provided by fixtures set into the sides every ten meters, just enough light to see ones footing. Ahead, almost at the low point, were the figures of two men.

As they came up on them, McKernan recognized one as Entwhistle. He didn't know the other.

"The body is in there," Entwhistle, said pointing at a metal cabinet set into the side of the tunnel. "Hsu, here, was conducting the search like you asked when he found her. The cabinet is a junction box for the electrical in this part of Hut Town. There's a breaker panel and some cross connects, but there's still plenty of room inside."

The front of the cabinet consisted of a double door that when opened would provide access to the entire width of the enclosure. At the moment they were shut.

"When I saw the body inside, I shut the doors and then called my boss," Hsu said. "I really didn't want to have to look at it while I waited. This place is creepy enough as it is without a corpse staring at you."

"That's fine," McKernan said, trying to sound as if he understood. "I'm going to open them now. You can step back out of sight if you like."

Hsu stepped back a couple of paces. McKernan turned the handle and opened the door. Slumped against the back of the cabinet was the body of a black woman, a little on the pudgy side, and probably in her mid thirties if McKernan was any judge. She was dressed in a tight fitting, low cut, red dress that had been torn at the top. Judging from the breast that was hanging out there could be little doubt of the gender, though it was possible the breasts had been artificially augmented. The body was in much better shape than the first corpse. It didn't escape McKernan's notice that the woman's hair had been bleached blonde. He also noted the bruising around her neck. She had been strangled just like the first victim.

"Are these cabinets locked?" McKernan asked.

"No. What's the point?" Entwhistle said. "There really is nothing inside to steal. If it's any help, Inspector, I checked the records on this box. It was serviced a little over three months ago. One of the breakers had tripped and had to be reset."

"I take it there was no sign of a body at that time?" McKernan asked.

"No," the power supervisor said. "It would have been reported."

"Sorry," McKernan said with a smile. "Just a bit of gallows humor. Actually, that's a very important bit of information. I'd appreciate it if you could send the service record to us."

"I'll do it right now," Entwhistle said, tapping on the computer tablet that hung from his belt.

"Hsu, is it?" McKernan asked. "Did you see anything unusual before you opened the cabinet. Footprints? Anything like that? Anything that didn't belong?"

"I came in from Corridor B. There were lots of footprints, but that's kind of normal. This tunnel gets a lot of traffic. But coming from C it almost looked as if the middle of the walkway had been swept."

"Or a body had been dragged?"

"Yeah, maybe," Hsu agreed.

"Nothing else?"

"Not that I noticed. The light isn't very good down here."

"Well, thanks. I don't think you or your boss need to hang around here any longer. We'll take it from here."

"Do you want my men to keep searching, Inspector?" Entwhistle asked.

"Yeah, George. I think they better," McKernan answered with a sigh.

"How many more bodies are you expecting to find?"

"I wish I knew. I really do," McKernan replied sadly.

"Well, you might as well get to work, Gaeretts. Pictures of everything. Get some of the dust on the walkway leading towards C. We probably messed it up on the way in, but you never know."

After the two power plant workers had left, Gaeretts asked, "Do you think the victim was murdered elsewhere and dragged down here to hide the body?"

"It certainly looks like it," McKernan said. "Judging from her clothing, she might have put up a struggle, too. The doc will be able to tell us."

"Working girl?"

"Dressed like that? More than likely. Half the bars and bordellos in Hut Town are just the other side of that lock. Our killer could have gotten her alone for a little private grope, maybe inside the airlock. Once inside, he strangled her, dragged her through the hatch into the tunnel and stuffed the body in the first convenient place of concealment."

"I bet she put up more of a struggle than the first one," Gaeretts remarked. "She must go eighty, ninety kilos."

"Yeah. She wouldn't be easy to drag once she was unconscious or dead, either. Our killer must be one strong hombre."

"Think he planned it?" Gaeretts asked as he took a picture of the corpse.

"Maybe. Hard to say. Might know more after the autopsy. Speaking of which, better give a call to Ferris or whoever is available and get a cart to haul the corpse to the hospital. I sure don't want to try to carry her."

"You can say that again. Even on Mars she's no light weight."

"Finish up the pictures, see if there are any prints. I'm going to walk the tunnel to see if I can spot anything while you're at it."

McKernan walked the length of tunnel both ways from corridor to corridor. The only thing that he found was a small bit of red fabric that had caught on a sharp piece of metal just outside the hatch into corridor C. It looked to be a match to the dress of the victim. He put it in an evidence envelope and waited until Ferris showed up with a cart.

Chapter 16: Post-Mortem

It was after 18:00 when they wheeled the corpse into the hospital. The physician on duty was Dr. Greenwood. McKernan knew him slightly from past encounters. He was in his late thirties and in the first year of his second three year stint on Mars. His sarcastic manner concealed a core competence. Despite his sometimes abrasive attitude, most of his patients seemed to like him.

"What have you got there, Inspector? Greenwood asked upon seeing the plastic sheet draped over the cart. "Did one of you constables go too far with a drunk?"

"We've got what we think is a murder victim, Doc," McKernan said, the tone of his voice indicating he was in no mood to be joked with. "I need a death report ASAP. An ID would be good, too."

"Wheel it into the surgery and let's take a look," Greenwood said, setting the cup of coffee he had been drinking on the reception desk.

They pushed the cart through the swinging doors of the surgery and up against the examining table. The physician pulled aside the sheet. There was a moment of hesitation when he saw the face. McKernan tried to read his expression, but wasn't sure whether it was surprise or something more.

"Christ!" Greenwood exclaimed. "It's Lola."

"You knew her?" McKernan inquired.

"Not that way, Inspector, if that's what you're thinking. Her name is Mabel Johnson. Lola was her working name. She was a patient of mine. I've seen her off and on for the last two years. Usual stuff. The last time was about five months ago. Somebody had beat her up. She had a black eye and some bruising around the ribs."

"I don't remember getting a report of anything like that." McKernan stated.

"You wouldn't have. The working girls tend not to like attracting the attention of your constabulary. Force of habit, I expect. Lola asked me not to file a report."

"You're supposed to report any assaults."

"I'm supposed to do a lot of things, Inspector. Mostly I just try to take care of my patients. Now can we stop arguing irrelevancies. I need some help getting the body on the examining table. Lola always did carry a load."

Between the doctor, Gaeretts and McKernan they managed to shift the body onto the examining table.

"Sheesh, she's cold as ice. How long has she been dead?"

"I was hoping you could tell me that, Doc," McKernan said. He explained the circumstances of discovery of the corpse. "So far, all I can tell you is that it was probably sometime in the last four months. I was hoping you could give me a more exact answer."

"Not expecting miracles, are you?"

"At this point even the right week would be helpful. Even the month."

"You think Lola's death is related to your mystery boy?"

"Maybe. Two bodies hidden in the same part of Hut Town. I'm not a big fan of coincidences."

"Oh, well. It's a slow night. Leave her with me and I can probably have a preliminary report for you in a couple of hours."

"That would be great, Doc," McKernan said.

"Yeah, don't mention it. The sooner you get out of here, the sooner I can get to work."

Leaving the hospital, McKernan thought about calling Beth, but decided he didn't want to inflict his mood on her. Deciding on a drink instead, he headed to Finnegan's.

Finnegan was behind the bar as usual. A couple of guys he recognized as engineers occupied one of the table. Otherwise the place was empty. McKernan sometimes wondered how Finnegan managed to keep the place open.

"What can I get you, Chief Inspector?" Finnegan asked as McKernan grabbed a stool.

"Whisky, straight up."

"This about the corpse they found out in Hut Town?"

"How'd you hear about that?"

"This is Mars, Inspector. News travels fast and it's hard to keep a secret."

"I don't know about that. I seem to be running into enough of them."

"Well, I've got something for what ails you." Finnegan put a tumbler on the bar and grabbed a bottle from the top shelf of the back bar. It was Scotch, McKernan noticed, from Scotland, even. Finnegan poured two fingers of the amber liquid in the glass. He popped the cork back in and was about to replace it on the shelf but thought better of it. He got out another glass and poured a measure equal to the one he had poured for McKernan.

"As long as the word is out, do you want to talk about it?" Finnegan said after his first sip.

"Working girl. Went by the name of Lola. Her body was found in an electrical cabinet in one of the cross tunnels out at the end of Hut Town."

"Murdered?"

"Probably, there were signs of strangulation."

"You seem to be taking it personally," Finnegan observed, shaking his head.

"Let's just say I don't like the idea of people being killed on my watch. The thing is, I've now got two cases where people went missing and the first my department hears about it is when the corpses turn up months, maybe even years later. Mars isn't that big of a place. Makes me wonder how many more bodies are going to turn up."

"You shouldn't take it to heart. You have to understand, Inspector, that to a lot of the people out in Hut Town you are the face of the Trust Authority. They see you as representing the mining companies and the people with money."

"Tell that to the governor," McKernan said. "He thinks I'm suspect because I live out there."

"That's the curse of being an honest cop, Inspector," Finnegan said reflectively. "Neither side trusts you."

"Yeah. That sounds about right."

"Care for another?"

"No. I'd better not. I'm waiting for the report from the Doc."

"Cup of coffee, then? A glass of water? I can fix a ham and cheese sandwich if you're hungry."

"A sandwich and coffee sounds good. I haven't eaten since lunch, and that was a soy dog."

"Those things will kill you," Finnegan said with a smile.

He ate the sandwich slowly watching the time go by. He was rethinking having another drink when he got a text from Greenwood asking him to come to the hospital.

"Put it on your tab?" Finnegan said as he got up to leave.

"Yeah." McKernan, like all Trust Authority employees, got a monthly shipping allowance which meant he could import goods from Earth without paying the freight. His allowance was a generous two and a half kilos. Most of it went to settle tabs with various businesses who then aggregated allowances to bring in stock that couldn't be produced locally. McKernan's monthly tab at Finnegan's typically ran to a half kilo.

Greenwood was still working over the body when he got to the surgery.

"You got something for me?" McKernan asked.

"I don't know how useful it will be, but she's been dead a minimum of two weeks, probably longer. Personally, I'd take odds on nearly three months. The cause of death was strangulation. Bare hands. Whoever did it was a strong fucker, too. I took some measurements and compared them to the post-mortem of your Jane/John Doe. It could be the same guy. I'm not saying that it is, but it could be."

"Thanks, Doc. At least I may only be dealing with one homicidal maniac."

"She'd had intercourse within twenty-four hours of her death, but that's not particularly surprising. I searched her clothing, too, what there was of it. I don't think robbery was the motive. I found two hundred dollar bills tucked into her bra."

"So a homicidal maniac who isn't a thief."

"One other thing. I took some blood and did a quick tox screen. I found something interesting. There were traces of a new synthetic drug. I won't bore you with the technical name, but on the street in L.A. it goes by the name Code Blue. It's becoming the favorite date rape drug."

"How did you know to look for it?"

"Hunch, partly. Mostly because it's easy to test for. It's fairly stable and doesn't break down in the system like a lot of these drugs. It doesn't break down at all if the person is dead. The only way it leaves the body is by elimination, by which I mean pissing it out. Without knowing how much she was dosed with I can't tell for sure, but I'd say Lola was drugged within a few hours of when she died. The drug wouldn't have knocked her out, but would have made her easy to manipulate. That would make a difference with a woman Lola's size. She could be feisty when she was mad."

"Great, now I have to worry about drugs, too."

"Maybe not so much, Inspector. Somebody managed to bring in about a hundred doses of the stuff about four, five months ago. A few of the working girls complained to me about it. I tracked down the guy who had been selling it. Convinced him to turn the remains of his stash to me."

"And you didn't report it?"

"The guy would have lost his job and been sent back to Earth where he would be unemployable. I thought it would be better to get the drug out of circulation than to ruin some shlubs life. The good news is that only about six doses are unaccounted for."

McKernan started to object to the doctor's actions, but stopped. The problem was, McKernan half agreed with Greenwood's decision. "Any chance this drug was used on the first victim?"

"I doubt it. It's only been out on the street for maybe eight months, and I've only seen the one batch here on Mars."

"OK. Let me know if you see any more signs of it. No excuses. Anyone who has it may be the killer. Understand?"

"I understand, Inspector."

McKernan left and headed home.

CHAPTER 17: LUNCH AT THE MARS CLUB

When he arrived at the station the next morning, the first thing he did was ask Ortiz to see if she could track down Mabel Johnson's movements before her death. As was typical, the constable replied that she was already working on it. Not for the first time, McKernan reflected that he was going to miss her when she returned to Junction 3 after the baby came and she resumed patrol duties. As a detective she was a natural.

Greenwood's full report on the post-mortem was waiting on his computer. He read through it, but there wasn't anything new that they hadn't gone over the night before.

Also waiting in his computer's inbox was an invitation to lunch at the Mars Club. It was from Otis McAndrews, the local head of Anglo-Martian Mining. Unlike the local managers of most of the mining companies who tended to rotate through on a one or two year assignment before returning to Earth, McAndrews had been on Mars longer than the Inspector. Because of that, he had become the de facto spokesman for the mining interests. An invitation to lunch with him was not so much a request as an order, even if it was a polite one.

McKernan wondered what McAndrews wanted. He was a good man, a vocal proponent of granting some degree of locally accountable government, but he also was the head of one of the largest of the mining concerns. As such, his primary concern was with how events affected the corporate bottom line. The only major case that was new was the discovery of the two bodies, and he didn't see how that would be a big item to the companies.

Well, McKernan thought, there was only one way to find out. He responded with an acknowledgement. At least he'd get a free meal out of it.

The invitation had been for 13:00. McKernan arrived a few minutes early. The Mars Club was located on the main concourse between the Mars Hotel and the Sheraton just opposite from Finnegan's. The only outward presence was an airlock hatch set into the silica brick of the wall. A small polished steel sign with the words "Mars Club" etched in it sat discretely to one side of the hatch above a small button. Only once before had McKernan passed through that hatch. McKernan pressed the button.

The hatch popped open in response and the Inspector stepped through. Passing through the far side of the airlock was like stepping into another world. Almost quite literally. The décor of the Mars Club was modeled after a private London club of the first half of the twentieth century. If the walls of the club were of silica bricks, the fact had been hidden behind a tasteful combination of what looked to be plaster and oak trim. The fixtures were brushed aluminum and Art Deco in style.

McKernan found himself in a small vestibule facing a high, oak paneled desk, behind which stood an impeccably groomed individual in a conservative business suit. He was wearing a tie with discrete red and black diagonal stripes. McKernan tried to remember when the last time had been that he had seen someone wearing a tie.

"Chief Inspector," the man said, "Mr. McAndrews is expecting you. If you will come this way."

He found himself being led through the lounge, down a corridor towards the back of the club. Knocking discretely at a wood paneled door, his guide ushered him into a small, private dining room.

McAndrews rose from where he had been sitting at a round dining table and offered his hand. "I'm so glad you could join me, Erik. Please have a seat."

McKernan noted that the table was set for two. He took the seat offered.

"You may leave us now, Fenton," McAndrews said. McKernan's guide withdrew, shutting the door behind him."

"First, Erik, I'd like to say that the members were very pleased with the way the incident at Station Alpha was handled. It was best for all concerned that scandal was avoided. William MacKensie was a dear friend of mine. We were both much younger men when we came to Mars. The accident was a great tragedy. I'm glad that nothing has affected his reputation."

"I understand that he was not well at the end," McKernan said. "He probably would not have lived much longer in any case. I came to have a great deal of respect for the man in the short time I knew him."

"As I said, your efforts are appreciated."

He was interrupted by a tap on the door. A waiter wheeled in a cart and began to place food on the table.

"I took the liberty of ordering for you," McAndrews apologized. "I don't think you will be disappointed. The chef at the club is quite good."

"Wine, sir?" the waiter asked.

"Please," McKernan responded. The waiter filled his glass from a decanter and then did the same for McAndrews.

"I'm afraid that shipping costs force us to have all our wine delivered in plastic pouches rather than bottles. Still you'll find it a respectable vintage."

"Will that be all, sir?" the waiter asked deferentially.

"Yes, thank you. You can leave us now." McAndrews had the manners of a gentleman of an earlier century.

Lunch proved to be a small beef filet served au poivre with green beans and a salad served on the side. McKernan took a sip of the wine. As McAndrews had promised, it was "a respectable vintage."

"Eat up, Erik," McAndrews encouraged.

They ate in silence for ten minutes or so. The food was delicious.

When they had finished, McAndrews refilled McKernan's glass. "You are probably wondering why I asked you here."

"That had crossed my mind. I appreciate the lunch, but I am just a simple policeman."

"Not so simple, I think. How is the case of the corpse discovered in Hut Town coming?"

"Which one? The first or the second?"

"The first is the one I'm concerned with for the moment."

"Not very far, I'm afraid. The victim hasn't been identified, nor has the killer. I have suspicions as to the identity of the first, but no evidence."

"I understand one of your constables has been making enquiries back on Earth. This has caused some concerns in certain quarters."

McKernan was about to explain when McAndrews raised his hand.

"No, don't explain. I know your department is only doing its duty."

"I'd like to tell you a little story," McAndrews went on. "I'll name no names, so there won't be any misunderstandings."

"There is a certain Latin American businessman named Anthony. His family, which is an old one, though of uncertain origins, was prominent in mining circles and quite well off. This gentleman married a lovely young woman, a dancer, of the respectable sort I've been assured. Ballet, I believe. In due course they had a son and were quite happy. Unfortunately, tragedy struck. The woman was killed in an automobile accident, leaving the husband and a young boy. The youngster was of course given the best of educations. He was quite intelligent, I believe. Physically, he took after his mother, who had been quite petite. He was, shall we say, of an artistic temperament."

"This disturbed his father, who, though he loved his son, was full of Latin machismo. He did not approve of his son's artistic nature. He conceived of a plan where he would send his son off to one of his family's mining concerns with the hopes that in such an environment he might become, shall we say, more manly."

"The plan proved unwise. The son resented being packed off to what amounted, at least in his mind, to a prison. He escaped. His father's agents searched for him, but in vain. In time, he was given up as dead. To save face, the story was given out that the son had died in an accident. A funeral was held and 'remains' were cremated. And there matters stood."

"Now I'm sure that you can see that if, somehow, remains were to be discovered later that were alleged to be of the son, it would bring up painful memories to the family and might cause irreparable harm to the reputations of the family and the business. Furthermore, even if they were the actual remains of the son, it would serve no purpose to reveal them as such. The son would still be dead."

"What would you have me do, sir?" McKernan asked. "I've got a body. Actually, now I've got two, and I'm pretty certain they were killed by the same person. And I'm afraid that by the time this is done, I might have more on my hands."

"Erik, I'm not asking you to drop your investigation. By all means, find the murderer. Just don't bring the Guzman's name into it. It will do you no good."

"Is that a threat?"

"It's a cautionary warning. The Guzman family is a powerful one. Well connected. And remember, Rio Plata is a third world company. There are a lot of countries in the U.N. that would back them just to discomfort the West."

"I can continue the investigation as long as I keep Guzman's identity out of it?"

"Under those terms you will have my complete support, Erik. And the support of all the mining companies."

"Can you assure me that Guzman had nothing to do with the death of Mario Guzman?"

"Yes. Trust me. He loved his son."

McKernan drank the last of his wine. "You know that Mario didn't die right away? He laid in that tunnel for hours gasping for breath until he froze to death. I don't care what he was, he didn't deserve to die like that. No one does."

"Erik," McAndrews said soberly. "I know what he did was bloody stupid. The boy had no business being on Mars. If Anthony Guzman had thought with his head instead of his machismo he would have packed the boy off to Paris or London or Barcelona to be forgotten, and married a pretty young thing to sire him another son. In the end, everyone would have been much happier. But he didn't. And dragging Mario's corpse out of the closet isn't going to bring him back."

"I'll try to keep it quiet, sir," McKernan said. "As long as the investigation isn't compromised. But I make no promises."

"That's all I can ask, Erik."

"As it turns out the second body pretty much rules out Guzman's family having anything to do with his death," McKernan said.

"I knew that you would see it my way. Can I offer you some more wine?"

"No," McKernan answered. "I've got a murderer to find. Thanks for the lunch. I think I can find my way out." He rose and left.

Chapter 18: The Chief Inspector's Bad Mood

Despite the excellent lunch, Chief Inspector McKernan was in a bad mood when he returned to the police offices. He had never liked being told what to do, which, in effect was what McAndrews had just done. It wasn't that he didn't believe the story he'd been told. It had the ring of truth about it, and McAndrews had never lied to him before. It was that political pressure was being brought to bear on his investigation and he was powerless to do anything about it. Not if he wanted to keep his job.

For this reason he was less than sympathetic when Ortiz said, "I'm still hitting a brick wall in Montevideo, sir. They won't respond to my enquiries. Can't you use your influence to get them to cooperate?"

"No, Constable," McKernan said curtly.

"But, sir. The more they try to cover things up, the more I'm convinced that our victim was Mario Guzman. What reason would they have not to cooperate if Guzman had died in an accident? It just doesn't make sense."

"Look, Ortiz. I want you to forget about Guzman. That's a dead end. Even if our victim were Guzman, it's a cold case more than two years old. Half the people who were here then probably aren't even on Mars any more. We aren't going to get any useful leads out of it, and certainly not from Montevideo. I want you and Gaeretts to concentrate on Mabel Johnson. I want to know when she went missing, who she knew, everything about her."

"But, sir," Ortiz protested.

"Mabel Johnson is your only concern. Do you understand, Ortiz?"

"Yes, sir. I understand. Mabel Johnson," Ortiz answered looking like a whipped puppy.

"Good," McKernan said before storming into his office. He would have slammed the door, but he knew from experience that that would break the flimsy partitions that served as walls.

Once inside his office McKernan cooled down. He regretted the fact that he had lost his temper with Ortiz. She was a good cop trying to do her job. Just as he was.

At least part of what he had said to Ortiz was right. The story McAndrews had told him eliminated one line of reasoning. They didn't have to worry about why or how the boy had gotten to Mars. And Mario Guzman had probably not been killed by either his father or some member of his extended family trying to enhance their inheritance. His death had been a crime of sexual violence, just as had that of Mabel Johnson.

Assuming that the two crimes were related, and that was still a big assumption, it did give them something to work with. The killer was someone who had been on Mars two years earlier when Guzman was killed and had still been on Mars three months ago when Mabel Johnson had met her death. A majority of the men and women on Mars were there on a three year employment contract. When one accounted for people who signed up for a second stint and the relatively small number of more or less permanent residents, that meant that every year approximately one fifth of the population of Mars returned to Earth. In the two years that had elapsed between the murder of Guzman and that of Mabel Johnson, that would amount to roughly twenty thousand potential suspects who could be eliminated, nearly half the population of Mars. It wasn't much, but it was progress of a sort. At least it was something a policeman could understand, McKernan thought. He felt better.

A little after 16:00 there was a discrete knock at the door of McKernan's office.

"Come in," he said.

It was Ortiz. "I've got some information on Mabel Johnson, sir."

"Good. What have you got?"

"She was born and grew up in Chicago. Twenty eight years old. She came to Mars two years ago on a standard recreational contractor agreement. Nothing particularly unusual in her record on Earth. A couple of arrests for prostitution, but no drug charges or other crimes. She seemed to like her work. At least she was good at it. I checked her bank balance. It was sixty three thousand at the last entry a hundred and five days ago. She was putting two to three thousand away every month, even after expenses. She would have gone back to Earth after her three year contract moderately well off."

That was unusual, McKernan thought. Most of the working girls ended up blowing most of their profits on drinking or recreational drugs.

"There were a couple of hundred dollars on her body," McKernan said.

"She played everything by the book," Ortiz continued. "Filed all the forms, had the mandatory physicals right on schedule. Her last one was fourteen weeks ago, Dr. Greenwood. She was scheduled for another one ten weeks ago, but she never showed up. That's not that unusual. I gather that the procedures for the physicals are kind of lax.

No one seems to get too upset if a working girl misses one or two."

McKernan just grunted.

"She was renting a cubicle out towards the end of Corridor C in a flop used by a lot of the working girls. She had paid her rent six months in advance to get a discount. She still had a month to go on the lease. When I talked to the landlord, she said that as long as the rent was paid, she didn't pay any attention to whether the girls came or went."

"Anything else?"

"From what I could get, she worked out of Singapore Sam's and a couple of other joints. No one cares to talk too much out there."

"I'd be surprised if they did. I'll send Gaeretts out to check out her flop, but I don't expect he'll find anything. Good work, Ortiz."

"Thank you, sir."

"And Ortiz—"

"Yes, sir?"

"I'm sorry I lost my temper, earlier. I was having a bad day. I shouldn't have taken it out on you."

"I understand, sir."

"Guzman is a dead end. I don't doubt that the body we found was Mario Guzman, but his family didn't have anything to do with his death. The problem is, the family is powerful and politically connected and would just as soon not have the story come out. I won't go into the details, but I think we're back to our original theory of some guy picking up what he thought was a girl and blowing up when he found out she wasn't."

"And you think the same killer is responsible for Mabel Johnson's death?"

"That's the weak link in the theory. There's no question of Johnson being anything other than a woman. She also didn't bear any physical resemblance to Guzman. She was big, well endowed, and black. The only thing they had in common was the badly dyed blonde hair."

"Not much to go on, is it, sir?" Ortiz said.

"No, it isn't," McKernan agreed.

Chapter 19: MUR-001 "Authorized Personnel Only"

After Ortiz had left his office, McKernan did a quick check of his comp tablet for messages. After reading one of them his mood brightened and a smile came to his face. He'd been trying to come up with an excuse to see Dr. Haestert and the message was just what he was looking for.

A quick call and the doctor was on his communicator.

"Hi, Erik," the doctor answered.

"Hi, Beth. Do you have any plans for dinner?"

"Tonight?"

"Yes."

"Just the usual in the commissary."

"I've got a better idea."

"Oh. What is it?"

"A surprise."

"Sounds intriguing."

"Good. I'll stop by at 18:00 then."

"My shift at the hospital ends at 17:00. Why don't you meet me at the entrance to the Women's Quarters? That will give me a chance to clean up."

"I'll be there."

The entrance to the Women's Quarters was an anonymous airlock hatch behind which were the dormitory cubicles for unattached female Trust Authority employees. Across the hallway was the matching hatch for the Men's quarters. The accommodations provided ranged from 3 by

5 meter rooms with shared baths for junior personnel to 5 by 5 with bath for senior officials. None could be considered spacious or luxurious. It was no wonder many of the residents sought other quarters as soon as they could be arranged, with many of them ending up in Hut Town.

McKernan arrived a few minutes early carrying a small plastic travel bag. He didn't have long to wait as the doctor emerged from the hatch promptly at 17:59. For once she wasn't wearing hospital scrubs, and instead was dressed in a neat sweater over a trim pair of slacks. She had taken her hair out of its usual pony tail and let it hang free. McKernan approved.

"Where are we going?"

"I told you, it's a surprise," McKernan answered with a smile. "Just follow me."

He led them on what appeared to be a random course through the labyrinth of hallways that made up the core of Mars City proper. After what must have been a kilometer, Beth had to admit she was hopelessly lost.

"You do know where we're going, don't you?"

"Trust me."

A little bit farther on they stopped before a non-descript hatch labeled "Lower Level." McKernan opened it, revealing a steep metal staircase.

"Down there?" the doctor asked uncertainly.

"Down there."

At the bottom of the stairs Beth remarked, "I didn't know Mars City even had a basement." The space she found herself in was a maze of piping, ducts and conduits. Corridors led off in all directions.

"They had to put the mechanicals someplace," McKernan responded. "Down is easier than up on Mars. You don't have to worry about insulation or shielding. It's down this way," he added pointing along one of the corridors.

After a hundred meters they arrived at a hatch on which someone had neatly stenciled "MUR-001 Authorized Personnel Only" in bold red letters. The doctor just looked at McKernan.

He opened the hatch and they stepped through.

"Good evening, Inspector," a man waiting just the other side of the hatch greeted them. "So glad you could make it."

"Hi, George. This is Dr. Beth Haestert. I brought a little contribution," Erik said, pulling out a plastic bag from the travel bag and handing it over.

"A smoked ham, wonderful," George said examining the contents of the bag. He placed it on a cart behind him alongside several similar offerings. "I'm sure we'll find a use for it at our next dinner. Would you and the lady like a cocktail? Alex has whipped up something special, he assures me. I haven't dared try one yet."

"Why not," McKernan answered. George filled two beakers with ice and a blue liquid. As he was handing them over, he asked, "Do you want to sit at the communal table or by yourselves?"

"I think by ourselves tonight."

"It's early yet. Take your pick."

A long table flanked by benches ran along the center of the narrow room. It seemed to have been constructed of the same material used to make room partitions. Arranged along each side of the room were an assortment of small tables with two, three, or four mismatched seats. In all, the place appeared to have seating for forty or so people.

The silica brick walls had been painted in bright, but somewhat amateurish murals of a Marsscape. Down in one corner someone had added the image of a little green man.

He was using a three fingered hand to thumb his non-existent nose at the viewer. The back third of the space seemed to be taken up with a mish-mash of stainless steel shelving and workbenches as well as some very odd pieces of equipment.

After they had seated themselves at one of the side tables the doctor asked, "OK. What exactly is this place?"

"It's the Mars Underground Restaurant #1. Actually, it's also the only one."

"It seems a little out of the way for a restaurant."

"It's not really so much a restaurant as a kind of private club. Members only. And technically, it doesn't exist. Just as you won't find this space on any of the city's blueprints."

"I still don't understand."

"You know what the food in the commissary is like. It was even worse when MUR was founded five years ago, and there were no real options. The Trust Authority and corporations hadn't made any provisions for private kitchens in any of the housing it provided for employees. In reaction, a group of people, foodies, amateur chefs, and some who were just tired of the commissary started to get together with whatever they could scrounge for spontaneous dinners. Mostly they used lab equipment. Needless to say, this was frowned upon by the management. Then one of the group found this place. As I said, it doesn't really exist. It's more of a dead space between the foundations of two buildings. They started to meet here for their dinners and gradually they equipped it with a more or less complete kitchen with cold storage and workspace. On a rotating basis members prepare a meal whenever they can scrounge, barter, raise or import the ingredients. One menu for all. Diners pay for their meal either by supplying ingredients or subsidizing their purchase."

"And you are one of the members?"

"More or less by accident. I was tracking down reports of items going missing from scrap bins when I stumbled on this place. It was a choice of either report it or join. I chose to join."

"You continually surprise me, Erik."

"Try your cocktail. Alex is a wizard with grain alcohol and artificial flavoring. He also has a strange sense of humor. You never know what to expect."

Beth took a sip from what she recognized as a standard 250 ml. beaker.

"That's—well—odd. But good. It's hot and cold at the same time and it doesn't taste at all blue. What's in it?"

"Your guess is as good as mine. Alex is a chemist for Anglo-Martian. You never know what he'll put in his drinks."

"What's for dinner? Or will that be a surprise, too?"

"The menu is displayed on that computer screen on the wall. It looks like there will be a soup, a fish course, a beef entre, and desert. George Hagenschmidt made the desert. That's a good sign. He's an astronomer at the observatory and great with pastries and chocolate."

"Really. Chocolate. I haven't had any real chocolate since I got to Mars. It's hard enough to find on Earth."

"You just have to know the right people," Erik said mysteriously.

The room was slowly filling up with most of the people holding one of the blue beakers. The center table filled up first with the overflow occupying the side tables. There was a good deal of conversation going on, as everyone seemed to know each other.

Promptly at 18:30 the man who had been playing host at the door took a position at the head of the table.

"I'd like to welcome you all tonight. I think we've got an interesting menu in store for us. I'd like to thank Alex for his latest creation. He calls it a 'Sapphire Star' and as you can see it's, well, blue. He didn't divulge the ingredients, though he did say jalapeno peppers were involved. Marcy is providing the first course which is a squash based soup using vegetables from her own garden."

At this cue several people came out of the kitchen area carrying trays from which they dispersed small bowls of soup to the diners.

"This is excellent," the doctor remarked after her first taste.

"Marcy makes great soups. She's an office manager for Anglo-Martian."

"So do you ever cook for these dinners?"

"Rarely. Mostly I help out and provide some of the ingredients. I've got contacts with some farmers in the outthere."

"Outthere?" the doctor asked out of curiosity.

"Essentially anything that isn't Mars City or the immediate environs," McKernan explained.

"I'm starting to realize there's a whole other Mars I didn't know existed."

After a moment of silence McKernan asked, "Would you like some wine?"

"Please."

"I didn't know what they were serving tonight," he said as he produced a bottle from the bag he had placed under the table. "So I picked this. It's a syrah-grenache blend. Pretty versatile." He unscrewed the top and poured some into each of their glasses.

"I see it doesn't have a label."

"Finnegan brings it in in bulk and bottles it here. He encourages recycling of the bottles."

"It's wonderful, Erik," she said after taking a sip. She noticed that many of the other diners had also brought bottles of their own which they were sharing with those around them.

The fish course came next, tank raised, but still good. This was followed by medallions of hanger steak served with root vegetables. The portions of protein were small but the vegetables ample. The meal finished with a desert, a small dense slice of chocolate cake.

Many of the diners lingered over the latter, though some helped with the clearing of the tables and washing up.

With the bottle empty, McKernan screwed the top back on and stuffed it back in the bag. "Are you ready for me to walk you back home?"

"You'd better," Beth said with a laugh. "I'm hopelessly lost."

As they were walking back to the Women's Quarters Beth said, "You found another body."

"Yes," McKernan said grimly. "This one appears to have been dead only a few months. We know who she was, too, this time."

"Dr. Greenwood showed me the corpse. He wanted to compare notes. Judging from the bruising on the neck we both agree that they were probably killed by the same man."

"We're operating on that theory, though I can't say it makes me any happier."

"Why?"

"If he's killed twice, there's a good chance he will kill again."

After that they walked in silence for a while. Then McKernan asked, "Do you know Greenwood well?"

"Only as a colleague, and at that we usually work different shifts. Why?"

"Just curious," McKernan responded.

"He's been here on Mars quite a while, hasn't he?" Beth asked. "Like you."

"Yeah, I think about five years. I get the sense that he's going to stay."

"You mean not go back to Earth?"

"Yes. He seems to be settling in from what I hear."

"And you. Do you think you'll ever go back to Earth?"

"Realistically, probably not. Not much for me there."

"Oh? Why?" the doctor asked.

"I don't really have any family left. My mother died when I was in the service. My dad died a few years later, just before I left for Mars. I've got a couple of nephews and a niece somewhere, but I've lost contact with them."

"What about your sister, or brother?"

"She died in the Thai flu epidemic the year before my mother died."

"I'm sorry."

"We were never that close. Different lives. Anyway, there's no one back on Earth and the job prospects for an ex-Martian policeman aren't that great. I'd probably end up as a U.N. commissioner someplace in the middle of nowhere."

"And is there anyone for you on Mars?"

"No. Or at least not yet," McKernan said with a shrug. "But at least I've got my job and some friends."

They found that they had arrived back at the hatch for the Women's Quarters.

"Thanks for the dinner, Erik. I had a great time." She reached up and kissed him on the cheek and then before he could say anything she had disappeared through the hatch.

Chapter 20: No Clues in the Flop

McKernan arrived at the police offices the next morning to find Ortiz and Gaeretts talking over a morning cup of coffee. This was getting to be a habit, and the Inspector admitted to himself that not only would he miss the constable's presence when she returned to her patrol duties, but having an extra body on call was proving useful. Normally he only had enough staff at Mars City; in addition to himself there was one man manning the desk while another walked the corridors. The rest of his force was scattered thinly over the planet's surface. It was less than ideal given the growing population, but it was all the Trust Authority would budget for.

With a mental shrug he asked Gaeretts, "Did you find anything of interest in Johnson's flop?"

"Not much. Mostly just her clothes and toiletries. As far as I could tell, there was no sign of a struggle. The landlord said she didn't allow the working girls to bring men back to their flops. She said it caused too much trouble. That was about all she said."

"Any chance Johnson kept a diary or anything like that?"

"Not that I could find. She did have a comp tablet. We were just looking it over when you came in."

"Anything on it?"

"Some trashy romance novels, or so Ortiz informs me," Gaeretts said with a laugh.

"Hey, a girl needs a little romance in her life," Ortiz defended.

"I'd say you had enough romance," Gaeretts said, pointing at the constable's swelling womb. He continued, "Some e-mails. She evidently was keeping in touch with relatives back on Earth."

"No list of clients?" McKernan queried.

"Not that we could find. But most of the action out there are miners coming in for a spree, not regulars."

"Yeah. I was hoping we'd get lucky and have a list of suspects to focus on."

"Sir." Ortiz said, "There is one other thing. We read through some of the personal e-mails. It seems Johnson has a kid back on Earth. A boy, about four. Her mother is taking care of him. It looks like Johnson was sending money back to her for the boy."

"Oh, hell," McKernan said.

"That's what she was doing on Mars, trying to get a stake so she could send the boy to a good school and could live in decent place," Ortiz said. They both knew from personal experience what it was like growing up without money. Mars might be rough, but compared to the slums of Earth it was a paradise.

"I was wondering, sir, what is going to happen to the money Johnson had in the bank?"

"Get an address for the mother off her tablet. I'll make sure that her kid gets the money. It may take a few months to get all the paperwork settled, but there shouldn't be a problem."

"Thanks, sir."

"Gaeretts, did you have any luck questioning any of the other residents in the flop?"

"Not much. A lot of 'what a shame' and 'Mabel was a good girl,' but not much in the way of information. They tend to be pretty tight lipped out at the end of Hut Town. Particularly with a cop. Too many of them know me."

Gaeretts had been part of the security force since before McKernan came to Mars. He wasn't a hardass, but over the years he had had to knock enough heads together to earn a reputation. So had McKernan himself, for that matter. Part of it was a holdover from Earth, the Inspector thought to himself, the age old antipathy between cops and those they had to police. He couldn't blame them. Most of the sex workers and honky-tonk staff came from the slums of Earth and had worked in those occupations before Mars. In those environments policing was a lot more about keeping people in line rather than protecting them.

"Makes it hard to get information, doesn't it?" McKernan commented.

"Sir, if I might make a suggestion?" Ortiz interjected.

"Yes?"

"Maybe if I went out there alone, tried to talk some of the working girls. They might open up more to a woman than a male police officer."

"Forget about it, Ortiz. I'm not going to send you out in, well, your condition."

"But that might be an advantage, sir. Whose going to be afraid of a pregnant woman?"

"I'm not going to risk it," McKernan said firmly.

"It might be the only way we can get a lead on this case, sir. Somebody must have seen something. Someone Johnson was with before she was killed. Even if we could pin down the last time anyone saw her, it would be a help. Maybe even someone remembers the kid."

"Look, I'm not saying it's not a good idea, Ortiz. Maybe we can bring the women from her flop here to the station so you can question them," McKernan said.

"I think it would be better if I did it away from the station on their home ground. Look, sir. I'm a trained policeman. I can take care of myself. I spent a year bouncing drunk spacemen on Luna when I was in the Air Police. And I'd be careful. Trust me," she said patting the bulge of her belly.

McKernan thought about it for a moment. It was a good idea. And he had to admit to himself if Ortiz wasn't pregnant he wouldn't be as hesitant.

"OK. I'll let you do it. But you go armed, and you check in with me or Gaeretts every fifteen minutes when you're out there. And only in the day time."

"Yes, sir. I'll play it safe."

"Good. I want you to coordinate it with Gaeretts and I want Ferris or whoever else is on patrol in the area at all times. Do I make myself clear? To both of you?"

"Don't worry, Chief. I'll look after our little girl here," Gaeretts said. Ortiz punched him in the arm, being none too gentle about it.

Chapter 21: A Break in the Case

The next several days were quiet ones. Dr. Haesterts schedule at the hospital precluded any lunch or dinner dates to McKernan's annoyance. Ortiz was out asking questions in Hut Town. He found that he missed her presence in the station. Gaeretts had never been much of one for conversation. The Chief Inspector had even managed to catch up on his monthly and quarterly reports, the budget requests, and even the department accounts. He found himself looking again and again at the reports of the two murders, but nothing new presented itself.

It was almost with relief, then, when he received a call from Ortiz.

"Where are you, Ortiz? I thought I told you to check in."

"I thought that was what I was doing, sir. I'm out at the end of Corridor C."

"OK. Is everything all right?"

"No problems, sir. But I think I've found someone you should talk to. She might have a line on the killer."

"Good work, Constable. Bring her in and we can see what she has to say."

"That's just it, sir. I don't think she'd be very comfortable talking to you at the station. Gaeretts was right, people out at this end of Hut Town don't really trust figures of authority. Nothing personal, sir. I think it's just force of habit left over from Earth. I tried to assure her that she wouldn't get in trouble, but she doesn't want it getting around that she was getting close to the police."

"Kind of hard to keep that sort of thing secret in Mars City."

"Yeah, I know. But I thought maybe if you met her someplace discrete, she might open up to you."

"OK. Where do you suggest?"

"Do you know the 'Tea Room?' It's out towards the end of Corridor D. Some of the working girls go there when they want to get away."

"I'm not familiar with the place. I'm not much of a tea drinker. But I can find it. It's hard to get lost in Hut Town."

"Can you meet us there in half an hour, sir?" Ortiz asked.

"I'll be there."

The original settlement on Mars, that odd collection of inflatable structures that was to become Hut Town, was arranged in five parallel rows running roughly north and south for several kilometers in the Martian sands. Of these, Corridor C was the oldest, and therefore the least desirable. The huts there, except at the far end, were the earliest and smallest model, basically a shell that had first been inflated and then had expandable foam sprayed on the inside to stiffen the skin and provide a modicum of insulation. They had been laid out on either side of a central tube that provided access from one building to another without having to don a surface suit.

Hut Town had grown in a haphazard manner, with new structures being added at the ends of the corridor. Eventually, this arrangement had proven unwieldy and additional corridors had been built to either side of the initial row of huts. As these huts were newer models with improvements based on experience these newer corridors became more desirable and the huts along Corridor C were relegated first to support roles and then later to the first entrepreneurs. When the first more or less permanent construction of Mars City was built at the south end of the corridors, this came to be even more the case as most of the government and corporate functions moved to permanent quarters within the silica brick walls of the new construction. Thus was hut town born. Only later had it become capitalized.

Corridor A, the westernmost of the five, was adjacent to the landing field and was still given over mostly to the workshops and service functions related to the field. Some of the pneumatic structures there had even been replaced by permanent construction as corporations found it cheaper to build new silica brick structures than to maintain the older huts. On the other side of Hut Town, Corridor E was likewise given over to corporate uses such as vehicle maintenance and what manufacturing was carried out locally. Corridors B & D were mostly given over to residences, except at the ends where there was some retail and commercial space. This is where those people who chose not to live in the U.N. or corporate dorms lived, including McKernan himself. Which left Corridor C in the middle, with the oldest and most uncomfortable huts and the cheapest rents and some of the most dubious residences, especially at the far end of the corridor.

Which is not to say that these rules were hard and fast. People looking for space, whether for business or residential purposes, tended to grab whatever became available regardless of location. The exact ownership of Hut Town was a matter of some contention. The huts had been erected by a variety of entities, various nations, businesses, educational institutes, the Trust Authority. Often, when these entities had moved into more permanent quarters the huts had just been abandoned to be occupied by whoever was quickest. The exchange of possession of huts occurred on whatever terms were mutually agreeable to both parties. There was no such thing as a clear title, except, perhaps, for some of the corporate facilities.

All this crossed McKernan's mind, not for the first time, as he headed out towards the meeting. One of these days, he suspected, the issue would come to a head, particularly if the Trust Authority, realizing its diminishing relevance, tried to reassert its power over a population that was becoming with time less dependent on the supposed largess of Earth. Oddly enough, it was one issue where the big corporations tended to side with the residents of Hut Town rather than Trust Authority.

McKernan was unfamiliar with the Tea Room. He realized that he rarely got out to the far end of Corridor D. His own hut was on Corridor B and most police activity occurred in the de facto red light district at the end of Corridor C. He needn't have worried, the place was clearly marked with a sign in neat black letters proclaiming "Ye Olde Tea Room" over the entry hatch. He wondered if the name had been intended as a joke or if the operators were serious.

Entering through the hatch, he found a brightly lit space with a half dozen tables, each surrounded by a set of chairs. Towards the rear was a counter which bore a collection of pastries as well as the various apparatus for supplying coffee and tea.

Ortiz was sitting at one of the tables. It was the first time that he had seen her when she wasn't wearing either her uniform or a surface suit. It was also apparent that the baby was due at almost any time. She was with a woman that McKernan didn't recognize, someone thin, who looked to be in her late thirties or early forties, but was probably younger. She had a face that resembled those he'd seen in photographs from the dust bowl in the twentieth century. She was not what one would call attractive, but then the attractive ones had no need to leave Earth. She also had shockingly red hair.

"Mary, this is Chief Inspector McKernan. He wants to ask you a few questions. You can trust him. Inspector, this is Mary."

She smiled nervously as he sat down. A waitress came over to take their order.

"I'll take a cup of coffee, black," McKernan said. The women had tea.

"Would you like a plate of cakes? You only have to pay for what you eat," the waitress said helpfully.

"That would be nice, thank you," McKernan said trying to put Mary at ease.

The waitress brought their order. The water for the tea came in an actual ceramic teapot. The cakes looked appetizing, as well, little squares of pastry with a white frosting. Mary took one of the cakes and nibbled on it daintily.

"Now, Mary, what is it you have to tell me?" McKernan asked after she had finished a cake and had put another on her plate. Discretely he turned the record function of his comm unit on.

Chapter 22: Evidence in a Tea Room

"First, maybe I should tell you how I found Mary," Ortiz said. It was clear that she wasn't sure how comfortable her witness would be opening up with the inspector.

"Yes, I'd like to know that," McKernan responded trying to keep his voice reassuring.

"I had asked around about Mabel Johnson, but no one seemed to know much about her. But then I thought about her hair. It was obviously dyed, but there aren't any beauty shops on Mars that I knew of. I asked one of the girls who did her hair? She told me about Mary."

"So you dyed Lola's hair?" McKernan asked using the last victim's working name.

"Oh, yes. She really liked it. I do a lot of the girls' hair. You know it's like Elena said, there aren't any beauty shops on Mars."

"Did you study to cut hair?" McKernan asked.

"Yes, back on Earth, West Virginia. That's where I'm from. I went to cosmetology school for a whole year. But I couldn't afford to get a license. That was really too bad, because I like the work. I can cut hair really good. I can color it, too, except that it's really hard to get the chemicals here on Mars. I have to make do with what I can find. That's why the colors are a little off sometimes," Mary said a little self consciously.

"So you do the hair of a lot of the girls?"

"Oh, yeah. And not just the working girls, either. I do the hair for a lot of women in Hut Town. I can pick up some good money on the side. I'm thinking of opening up a real shop if I can find a cheap place."

"That sounds nice. And you did Mabel Johnson's hair?"

"Yes. She was one of my regulars."

"What can you tell us about Mabel? When was the last time you saw her? Was it when you did her hair?"

"Oh no. I'd see her around, you know, at Thelma's or some of the other places. We weren't like close friends, but we got along good."

"Did you know that she had been beaten up?"

"Yes. That was awful. It happens sometimes if you're not careful."

"Do you have any idea who did it to her?"

"She never said. But there was this guy hanging around her that night. I think he was the one that did it."

"Do you know who he is?"

"All I know is his first name was something French. Like Pierre maybe."

"Can you describe him?"

"He's a big guy. Not tall like, but strong, big shoulders, big hands. Like he could bend a metal bar. Brown hair, I think, but kind of short."

"Have you seen him around a lot?"

"Off and on. I think he's a prospector or something and only comes into town once in a while. He's been on Mars a long time, I know. At least as long as I have."

"And how long is that, Mary?"

"Almost three years. Gosh it seems longer." McKernan thought to himself that she had been around at the time of the first killing as well.

"Now I want you to think back, Mary. When was the last time you saw Lola?"

"Oh, geez. I don't know. I find it hard to keep track of time, you know. Like with the days being different lengths here and on Earth. It makes it really hard to keep track. I think it was about a week after Easter."

Ortiz and McKernan looked at each other. That would place it just about the time of the murder.

"Where was this? Where you saw her?"

"It was at Thelma's. I remember that."

"And was this Pierre guy there?"

"Now that you mention it, he was. I noticed him come in. He's hard to miss if you know him. Lola saw him, too. I know that, 'cause she left right away. That's why I think maybe he was the guy that beat her up."

"I want to thank you, Mary. You've been a real big help. We appreciate that. I'm going to ask Constable Ortiz to show you some pictures and see if you can identify this Pierre."

"I've already done that, sir."

"Why does that not surprise me?" McKernan said with a smile.

"I think there's something else you should hear, sir."

"What's that?"

"Mary, I want you to tell the Inspector about the boy," Ortiz said.

"That's a dead case, Constable," McKernan said in a warning tone.

"Not when you hear the full story," Ortiz said stubbornly.

"This had better be good."

"Go ahead, Mary."

"Well, it was a long time ago. Not too long after I came to Mars. Maybe two, two and a half years. I didn't know so many people back then. Just some of the girls that worked out of Thelma's."

"Anyway, I was just hanging out one day in Thelma's, sort of in the middle of the afternoon. This skinny little boy came in. He looked like he was maybe seventeen, eighteen, though I learned later he was a little older. He wasn't so much Hispanic as Latin like, and real handsome in kind of a delicate way. Almost pretty. He was scared. Real sacred, like someone was after him."

"Well, like I said, it was the middle of the afternoon. There weren't any customers around, just some guys drinking at the bar who weren't interested and a couple of the girls, so we got to talking to this kid. We were all wondering what the hell he was doing on Mars."

"He said his name was Mario. He could speak English pretty good. Probably better'n me," Mary said with a laugh. "He gave us this story about how his daddy who was some big shot on Earth didn't like him, was ashamed of him cause he wasn't macho enough. He had him shipped out to Mars to one of the mining camps to get rid of him. He'd been working at the camp, but he just wanted to go back to Earth. He said he wanted to be an artist, study in Paris."

"Anyway, the first chance he got, he stowed away on a land train coming to Mars City. When he got here he ditched his surface suit and had been hiding out for a couple of days, afraid that his daddy's men were going to come after him and drag him back to the mining camp. He didn't have any money. All he had was the clothes he was wearing. I don't know how he thought he was going to get back to Earth."

"We all felt sorry for him. You could tell he was a real sweet kid. He had this soft voice, and real polite, too. Well, he hadn't had anything to eat since he'd got there so we all chipped in and took him to a noodle shop and fed him a meal. One of the girls, I can't remember which one, took him to her flop and let him sleep there that night while she was working."

"Sure enough, the next day these guys come around looking for him. They had his picture and said they'd pay a reward if anyone knew where he was, but none of us would tell them."

"That night we got a bottle and went back to where he was staying to try to figure out what to do about it. It must have been the liquor, because we got this crazy idea to make him look like a girl. His hair was kind of long, anyway. So I cut and dyed his hair. He didn't need to shave. I'm guessing he'd had that fixed back on Earth. We shaved his legs and plucked his eyebrows, too. One of the girls who was about his size, like I say he wasn't that big, came up with a dress and panties. When we were done with him he could pass for a woman with no problem. Particularly on Mars."

"How'd he take this—makeover?" McKernan asked.

"He was reluctant at first, but then he went along with it. Kind of treated it like an adventure. I don't think he was gay, at least exclusively. At least Sheila, that's the girl whose flop he was sleeping at, said he wasn't."

"So what happened then? How'd he get by?"

"He hung around for a couple of weeks, dressed as a woman. He would hang out at Thelma's, just kind of in the background. Some of the guys that came in would buy him a drink or a meal. Don't get me wrong, it wasn't like he was trying to pick them up or anything, it's just that sometimes guys just want a little company and aren't too particular. The girls would try to help him out with food when they could. But I could tell after a couple of weeks he wasn't too happy about how things were going. I think he'd figured out there was no way he was going to get back to Earth."

"Anyway, one day he was just gone. I think we all figured that either his daddy's men had found him, or he'd gone back on his own. We didn't think anything had happened to him. That's what Elena said, that you found his body down in one of the tunnels underneath the corridor? Is that what happened?"

"Yes, I'm afraid so," McKernan said. "And the same thing happened to Lola."

"Such a sad story," Mary said, shaking her head.

"I want to thank you again, Mary, for telling us this. You've helped clear up a lot of details."

"Wait, sir," Ortiz said. "There's more. Mary tell the Inspector what else you told me."

"Well, the last night before Mario disappeared, he was in Thelma's. There was this guy who was buying him drinks. He was pretty drunk himself. He probably thought Mario was a woman. Let's face it, he was prettier than most of the working girls that were in there. Anyway, he kept asking Mario to go someplace where they could have sex. Mario kept saying he didn't want to."

"What happened then?"

"I don't know. Before anything happened, I'd picked up a john and we went back to my place. When I came back an hour or so later Mario was gone and so was the guy. That's all I know. If I had known what was going to happen, I would have told someone."

"You couldn't have known, Mary," McKernan said gently. "There was nothing you could have done."

"Tell him who the man was, Mary," Ortiz said.

"I can't be sure. It was a long time ago. But I think maybe the guy that had been buying drinks for Mario was Pierre."

Chapter 23: Suspect Identified

"Are you sure about that, Mary?" McKernan asked.

"No. I'm sorry, I'm not. Like I said, it was a long time ago. Over two years. I hadn't been on Mars long. I wasn't really thinking about it. I didn't know it would be important. It's just that I think it might have been him, the same guy I saw with Mabel."

"Don't worry about it, Mary. You've been really helpful, and we really appreciate it. If you remember anything else that might be useful, anything at all, however small, just give Constable Ortiz or me a call." He handed her one of his cards with his comm code. "And if you ever feel unsafe or threatened, let us know. Will you do that?"

"Sure, Mr. McKernan. And thank you for the tea and cakes. I'd better get going now if that's ok."

"Take care, Mary," McKernan said as she got up and left.

"What do you think, sir?" Ortiz said after she was gone.

"I think I'd like to have a talk with this Pierre. Have you been able to identify him?"

"I think so. At least when I showed his picture to Mary she said he looked like the guy. His name is Pierre Buche. He's a French-Canadian." She brought up his file on her comp tablet.

According to the file, Pierre Buche was a construction worker, not a prospector. He was employed by an engineering firm that had worked on various projects around Mars. That would explain why he had been in and out of Mars City over the last four years, which was how long he had been on the planet. He was listed as 175 centimeters, a couple of inches under six feet, but weighed a hundred kilos, well over two hundred pounds. From his picture it didn't look like any of it was fat. According to the file his record was clean, no arrests or charges back on Earth, nothing on Mars. His psych profile was normal, but that had been done five years earlier and a planet away.

"It might be him, or it might not," McKernan said after he had finished looking through the file. "Even if it is, all we have is a witness who may or may not have seen him sometime around the time when each of the last victims were seen."

"You don't believe Mary, sir?"

"Oh, I believe her, all right," McKernan said. "But even she, said she wasn't sure if it was the same man. It's hardly evidence, Constable. It's hardly even enough to take action on."

"So what do we do, then?" Ortiz asked, frustration in her voice."

"We, meaning you, do what good cops have always done in situations like this. Leg work. I want you to find out all you can about this Buche. Confirm where he was when we think our victims died. And keep asking around to see if anyone else remembers if they saw Buche with Mabel Johnson or Guzman. And if he's roughed up any of the other working girls. Does that make you happy, Ortiz?"

"Yes, sir."

"Good. And good work, Constable."

With a solid lead in hand, McKernan was in a good mood on his way back to the police station. Stopping at a food cart on the main concourse he bought sandwiches for Ortiz and himself. The pockets of pita bread were filled mostly with vegetables enhanced with a small portion of sausage, but were savory enough for both of them.

"Thanks, sir," Ortiz said. "I've been getting tired of the food at the U.N. commissary, particularly the diet that the doctor has me on because of the baby."

"You earned it," McKernan said smiling.

Once at the office, it didn't take Ortiz long to confirm that Buche had been in Mars City during the window of time that they thought both murders had occurred. But that, in itself, didn't prove anything. Even with the help of Mary's testimony, they couldn't narrow the date of either crime to less than the span of a week or so. Ortiz headed back out to Hut Town to see if she could find additional witnesses.

McKernan, for his part, brought up Buche's personnel file. He was, not surprisingly, a French-Canadian from northern Quebec. He had got his start in construction working for some of the energy companies locally and later up in the Canadian arctic. There was nothing in his record during that period to draw attention to him. Like many others, lured by the big money being offered by the corporations developing Mars, he had signed a three year contract with an engineering company. His work must have been satisfactory because the company had offered him a substantial bonus to sign up for a second contract. McKernan was familiar with his employer; they were as reputable and reliable as any on Mars. He had no reason to doubt the accuracy of what was in their files.

As was standard, he had taken a psychological evaluation before coming to Mars. Other than something of a quick temper, there had been nothing that had been flagged as a potential problem. Certainly, there were no signs of any sexually deviant nature. Of course, that had been five years earlier, and five years under the conditions of Mars could change a man, particularly a man who spent most of his time at isolated camps in the hinterlands.

He was unmarried, and there was no record in his personnel file of him having any long term relationship with a woman. On Mars, that wasn't at all unusual. With women heavily outnumbered by men, most men on Mars were bachelors. McKernan reflected that he, himself, was no exception.

The periodic performance reviews of his superiors at the engineering company didn't provide much information either. Adjectives like "strong" and "hard-working" were common. The image they provided was of a man who did his job competently if not brilliantly but who showed little initiative. After five years experience on Mars it was odd that Buche had not risen at least to the rank of foreman or team leader, but then, some people just weren't interested in taking on responsibilities. The only contrary note was a comment from one of his recent supervisors that Buche occasionally could be belligerent. Earlier reviews had described him as affable. Had something happened to make Buche change? Or was it just a personality conflict with that particular supervisor? There was no way to tell from the files.

His financial records produced little of interest, either. He was paid a substantial salary, at the high end for the type of work he did, but then with five years experience that was to be expected. He also seemed to have saved a higher than average portion of his wages. If Pierre Buche ever returned to Earth he would be, if not wealthy, at least comfortably well off.

McKernan felt the need to bounce his thoughts off someone else. Also, he admitted to himself, he was feeling a little lonely. He picked up his comm and called Dr. Haestert.

"Erik. Nice to hear from you. What's up?"

"I've got some new information about the killer. I'd like to talk it over with you. Are you free this evening?"

"Sorry, I don't get off until 20:00. One of the other doctors threw out his back and we're a little short staffed right at the moment."

McKernan thought for a moment. By 20:00 most of the restaurants would have stopped serving.

"I've got an idea. Why don't I make you dinner at my place? That will give me time to shop and start dinner."

"That sounds tempting. Can you really cook, or is this just a ploy to lure me to your lair?"

"I do ok. Certainly better than anything the commissary will be serving by the time you get off work."

"It's a deal, Erik. Unless something comes up here at the hospital."

He gave her directions to his place and then hung up.

Chapter 24: Chicken Paprikas and Watercolors

McKernan was busy cooking when the door buzzer sounded. A quick glance at the security camera's monitor showed that it was Dr. Haestert, still dressed in her hospital scrubs. Wiping his hands on a towel, he went to open the hatch.

"Hi, Beth. Glad you could make it. Did you have any trouble finding the place?"

"No. I think I must be getting used to Hut Town," she said with a smile. "What's for dinner? It smells great, and I'm famished. I haven't had anything to eat since lunch, and that was only a commissary sandwich."

The smells of simmering peppers and onions permeated the hut. "I'm making chicken paprikas," McKernan answered.

"You really can cook!" the doctor exclaimed.

"You haven't tasted it yet. Cooking on Mars has it's challenges. Like the air pressure, for one. I keep the hut at about the equivalent of a thousand meters above sea level. Water boils at a lower temperature. That can cause problems with things like pasta and noodles."

"I can imagine. Still, you seem to be coping."

"Finding certain ingredients can be difficult, too. Sour cream, for instance, which I needed tonight. None on Mars. But I know this guy who keeps a few goats to milk for cheese. He also makes some of it into yogurt. I'm hoping that will work as a substitute," he said with a shrug, changing the subject. "Care for a quick tour?"

"I'd love to."

"Well, this, as you can see," pointing to the three burner range and counter that occupied the portion of the hut closest to the hatch, "is the kitchen." An array of pots, utensils, and ingredients were stored on some makeshift wire shelving creating a compact but serviceable galley style workspace.

"Moving onward is the dining room," he indicated at table with two mismatched chairs, "and the living room." This latter was marked by a sofa, a worn looking chair that seemed to be made from a seat taken from a mars buggy, and a couple of shipping crates that served as end tables. A video screen was hung on the wall.

"It looks very functional," Beth commented. "And comfortable. That's an interesting picture," she said referring to a watercolor of a Mars scene that hung above the sofa. "Don't tell me you painted that, too?"

"No. That was painted by one of the scientists out at Station Alpha. It featured in an investigation I conducted. When the case was completed, Nils Jensen, the acting head of the station gave it to me as a parting gift. It's the view from out of the window of the recreation hall at the station."

"It's quite spectacular, really," the doctor said. "I'm afraid I really haven't had a chance to see much of the real Mars."

"There are some places that are actually quite beautiful. And some that are quite deadly," McKernan added. "I'll have to take you out, sometime."

"I think I'd like that."

"At the far end, I have my plants," McKernan said pointing to a collection of containers, pots, and grow lights that took up the third of the hut that was farthest from the hatch. "Let see, I've got tomatoes, peppers, beans, cucumbers, basil, and a number of other herbs growing at the moment."

"I think that's the thing I miss most about Earth, the plants," Beth said wistfully. "I know they have some potted bushes and things on the grand concourse, but it's not really the same thing, is it?"

"I guess not," McKernan agreed, though having grown up in one of the poorer parts of L.A. he hadn't really experienced much of nature. His later experiences in the jungles of Burma he'd just as soon forget.

There was a brief silence while the doctor looked around.

"OK. Am I missing something? Where do you sleep? Don't tell me you just use that couch?"

"No," McKernan said with a grin. "The bedroom is through here." He opened a hatch in one of the sidewalls of the hut. That led to a short tube and then another hatch which when opened revealed another hut the same size as the one they had just left. A comfortable looking bed took up much of the central portion of the hut. Several partitions of the ubiquitous plastic panels divided the space to make it cozier. There was even storage in the form of two doorless closets.

"There's a bathroom down at that end. It even has a shower and water recycler. At the other end I've got some more plants growing."

"This is amazing," Beth said with some degree of envy. "All this space. Are all the huts in Hut Town this luxurious?"

"No, but you'd be surprised at the ingenuity of some people. I got lucky a few years back when the guy who owned the hut next to mine was moving to the other side of the planet and offered to sell it to me. That's where we are now. All I had to do was put a lock between the two. Twice the space and redundancy on all the life support systems," McKernan said proudly.

"You know," Beth said, "these are the first quarters I've been in since I came to Mars that give any sense of a personality or permanence. The U.N. residence halls have all the charm of a college dorm."

"That's why a lot of people have moved out to Hut Town. It's not just that it's cheaper, though it is. But you can do what you want without having to deal with some bureaucracy. Not that it doesn't have its short comings. You have to pay for your air and power, or make your own. Radiation used to be a problem too."

"Radiation?"

"Cosmic rays, solar storms, that kind of thing. These old huts only have a thin metal skin and a couple of inches of foam insulation between the inside and space."

"Sounds dangerous. You said it used to be a problem?"

"Yeah, most of the huts used for living space have got roofs now. You build a superstructure of silica bricks or metal girders to support metal panels over a hut, and put a half meter or so of soil on top of that and it keeps out the worst of the radiation. Keeps them warmer, too."

"That's good to know," Beth said, shaking her head.

"Well, I should check on dinner. Would you like some wine?"

"I'd love some," the doctor replied. They went back through the hatch to the other hut where McKernan filled a couple of glasses with wine out of a box standing on the counter.

"Thanks, I needed that," Beth said as she took her glass.

"Rough day?"

"Just a lot of work being short staffed. Can I help with anything?"

"No, I think I've got things in hand. I started the noodles when you got here. It shouldn't be more than a few minutes before we can eat. I'll just taste the sauce." He dipped a spoon into the pan on the stove and tasted. Satisfied, he grabbed another spoon. "Would you like a taste?"

"Sure," she tasted, showing approval. "Either you really are a good cook or eating in the commissary has dulled my senses. What exactly is this, again?"

"Chicken Paprikas. Chicken cooked with onions and bell peppers and sour cream substitute and plenty of paprika."

He opened the refrigerator and brought out two small plates of slices of cucumber and tomato. "If you'll put these on the table, I'll dish up our dinner." He drained the egg noodles and placed them on two plates, put the chicken on top and added the sauce of peppers and onions on top.

"This is wonderful," Beth said, after the first few bites. "What is this with the cucumbers?"

"It's another Hungarian recipe. Just cucumbers and tomatoes with vinegar, salt, pepper and paprika."

"It's so fresh tasting."

"I picked the cucumber and tomato today."

"Of course. So how did you learn to cook?"

"I got tired of eating prepackaged meals and stuff out of pouches. I downloaded some cookbooks and just started cooking whatever I could. I've picked up some tips from people in the Underground Restaurant, but mostly I'm self taught."

"And the Hungarian thing. McKernan doesn't sound Hungarian?"

"It's not, trust me. One of the cookbooks I found was an old one of Hungarian recipes. It sounded interesting and exotic at the time. I just sort of picked up dishes from there.

They use a lot of things that I can grow myself which is good. I do a lot of Italian, too."

The rest of the meal was spent in small talk. McKernan was pleased that the doctor cleaned her plate. Finally finished, they sat back for a moment.

"You said there was something you wanted to talk over with me," Beth said, breaking the silence.

"Yeah. I think we've identified the killer, but I'm trying to figure him out. Why don't I refill our glasses and we can move to the living room and talk it over."

Chapter 25: Understanding a Psychopath

"I want you to listen to this," McKernan said, placing his comp tablet on the table in front of them. "It's a recording of an interview I had with one of the working girls in Hut Town. Her name is Mary, and she's something of a hair-dresser on the side."

The recording played with Dr. Haestert listening intently. McKernan had placed his comm so that it had discretely captured Mary's face as she talked.

"What do you think?" McKernan asked when the recording had finished.

"I think she's telling the truth," the doctor answered.

"So do I. Her story sounds plausible. From what checking we've been able to do, this Pierre, his full name is Pierre Buche, was in Hut Town around the time of both murders. He could have done it. He's certainly strong enough to have strangled them with his bare hands. The problem is that at the moment the only witness says she thought she saw him within a week or so of the killings and she thinks that he was the guy that beat up Mabel Johnson, but she doesn't have any sort of proof of that. It's not much to go on. It's certainly not enough to arrest a man on. It's barely enough to bring him in for questioning. I don't have access to any of the fancy forensic tools they have on Earth. If we had found fingerprints at either of the crime scenes I might have been able to use that, but we didn't."

"Yet you think this Pierre Buche is the killer."

"Yes. But that's based more on instinct than on fact."

"So what do you want from me, Erik? You said you wanted to talk this over. Why?"

"I'm out of my depth on this one. I'm just a cop, and maybe not even much of one by Earth standards. Most of the violent crimes I have to deal with are two drunks getting mad at each other and taking a swing. You throw them in a holding cell until they sober up and then send them back out to whatever mining camp they came from. With one exception, all the other serious crimes I've had to deal with were driven by greed, which is easy to understand. You follow the money, and you know where you are. Even that one exception was a case of passion. I could understand what motivated the killer. But this case—I don't know anything about psychopaths. It wasn't in the job description when I was hired. There aren't supposed to be any nut jobs on Mars."

"I'm not a trained psychiatrist, Erik. I'm basically a G.P. whose had a quick orientation course in hyperthermia and hypoxia and whatever else they thought was peculiar to the Mars environment."

"I know that, Beth. I'm not asking for miracles, just a little help. You might not be a psychiatrist, but you're probably as close as I'll get without having to deal with Earth."

The doctor took a sip of her wine. "OK. I did take a few courses in psychiatry, though I don't know how much good they'll be. They mostly dealt with depression, drug dependency, and things like that. Not abnormal psychology."

"Thanks, Beth. Any insight you can give me will be helpful."

"Just as long as you recognize I'm not an expert," the doctor qualified. "What do you know about this Pierre Buche's background?"

"He's a French Canadian. He was born in northern Quebec. Before he came to Mars he'd mostly worked construction in northern Canada at mining operations in places like Great Slave Lake, which, when you think about it is pretty good training for Mars; remote and harsh conditions. One of the companies that he worked for had contracts on Mars. They're always looking for qualified workers for their operations on Mars, and they offer big bonuses and good pay for those who qualify. Buche must have been attracted by the money."

"So he passed all the usual screening tests?" Beth asked.

"That's what the records say, and I have no reason to doubt them. The company he works for is reputable. They'd have no reason to cheat. Buche's job description calls more for muscle than brains or education. He knows his way around construction equipment, he can weld, use tools, that kind of thing, but he's not really any sort of high demand specialist. The company must have been happy with his work, though, because they gave him a hefty bonus for resigning at the end of his three year contract."

"So he's been on Mars a long time?"

"About five years."

"And he doesn't have any sort of a criminal record, either on Earth, or here on Mars?"

"Nothing that we've been able to find. There's never been a report filed by any of my people."

"What about his sexual partners? Is he married? In a long term relationship? Has he been in one in the past?"

"He's not married, and never has been. No long term relationship on Mars, but then, that's not all that surprising. There are even fewer women out at the mining camps, which is where he's been most of the last five years, than there are in Mars City. His records don't indicate anything on Earth, either, but unless he had applied for benefits for a partner there probably wouldn't be any record."

"And you know that he is heterosexual?"

"According to his file."

"Any problems at his job?"

"Like I said, the company seems happy enough with his work to resign him to a second contract. Most of his job evals indicate that he's a hard worker and good at what he does. Only one supervisor ever gave him a negative performance review. Described him as belligerent."

"And when was that?"

"A little over two years ago."

"Before or after the time you think that Mario Guzman was killed?"

"After. By a few months."

The doctor sat in silence for a while taking the occasional sip of her wine. McKernan left her to think while he cleared the table and cleaned up in the kitchen.

"So do you want a theory?" the doctor said when he was done.

"That's what I'm looking for."

"OK. And remember again I'm no expert."

"We've got a guy growing up in a small town, maybe even a village in northern Quebec. Isolated, insular, probably a pretty conservative environment. They're still mostly Catholic up there and take it seriously. He goes to work right out of high school or trade school working in construction. Again, mostly up in northern Canada at isolated mining camps. It's a pretty macho environment and still mostly male even in this age. So he probably never came into contact with anyone who wasn't, at least on the surface, strictly heterosexual.

"All that is fine. He seems to get along in that kind of life. But he never forms any sort of serious attachment to any women because there aren't many. Then he comes to Mars, the same sort of environment, except even more so. Still no problems. He's busy with his work, he's making lots of money, he gets into Hut Town every month or two, drinks a little, maybe engages a working girl for an hour or two, and then back out to work.

"Except once. He meets this cute looking blonde, buys her a drink maybe. Maybe she plays him up, maybe not. It might not matter, depending on how much he'd been drinking. He asks her to go to a flop with him. Maybe she says yes, maybe not. Maybe he just follows her out into the corridor when she refuses. He gets her alone in some dark corner. And then he discovers that she is a he. He figures he's been played for a sucker. He's been conned. Ridiculed. He gets angry. He finds his fingers around the blonde's neck. He squeezes. Hard. The blonde becomes unconscious. He panics and hides the blonde in the first place he can think of, the service tunnel under the corridor. He's not trying to hide the body for long, just long enough so that he can disappear and go back to work. He may not have even realized that his victim wasn't dead yet.

"He gets back to work and pretends nothing ever happened. The body isn't found, so it's not connected to him. But then the guilt starts to build up. Partly for having killed the blonde, but probably more for having fallen for what turns out to have been a man. And with the guilt comes the doubt. The doubt about himself. Had he really been attracted to the blonde because she was a man? He's probably been sexually repressed most of his life. It's the only way to cope with the environments he's been in. Maybe his personality starts to change. He becomes touchy, belligerent towards authority.

"Then it all starts to fade. Nothing happens. He never hears about the body in the service tunnel again. A couple of years go by. Then he sees Mabel Johnson. It doesn't matter that she's black and without a question a woman. Same color hair. It acts almost as a trigger. He lashes out, beats her up, then goes back to the camps. But next time he's back in Hut Town he tracks her down. She's afraid of him, tries to avoid him. It's hard to know what he was thinking at that point. Maybe he thought that if he could have sex with her he could put his demons to rest. Maybe he thought that he needed to kill her for rejecting him. Either way, he strangles her in some dark place and hides the body thinking it may never be found.

"That's my theory, Erik. It might be close to the truth, or it might be something only fit for a cheap novel. I don't know which. I'm not sure I could tell, even if I could talk to Buche face to face. I'm just not the right kind of doctor for that."

"I'm sorry I put you through this, Beth. It's not your problem, it's mine. But I think you've come as close to what happened as either of us can."

"You know what the problem is, though, don't you, Erik?"

"What's that?"

"Buche has killed twice already that you know of. And with Mabel Johnson, at least, he went out of his way to do it. There's one thing I remember from my coursework on serial killers, and it's this; once they start killing they don't stop, not until they're stopped. If he's killed twice, he's going to kill again. You've got to stop him, Erik."

"That's what I was afraid of," McKernan said, draining his glass. He thought of pouring himself another, but then thought better of it.

"It's getting late, Beth. Do you want me to walk you back to the women's quarters?"

"That won't be necessary. In fact, I don't have to leave at all. I've got the late shift tomorrow, and after my little horror story I'd just as soon not sleep alone tonight."

Chapter 26: A Rude Awakening

McKernan awoke feeling warm and relaxed. There was an arm draped over him and a body pressed up against his back. Unfortunately, the mood was broken almost at once by the buzz of his comm.

"This has better be good, Gaeretts," he said when he answered it.

"Sorry, Chief, but we found another body, and this one is fresh."

"Fresh?"

"As in the body is still warm, maybe only a few hours old."

"Where is it?"

"The farthest cross-connect between Corridors C and D. Ferris found her on his rounds about an hour ago." McKernan looked at the time on his comm. It was just before 0400.

"OK. I'll be there in a few minutes," McKernan said terminating the call.

"Erik, what is it?" the doctor said. McKernan could see her by the dim light provided by the life support display. She was sitting up now, the sheet clutched up around her chest.

"Another body has been found. I have to go."

"Of, course," Beth responded.

"There's no need for you to get up yet. You might as well go back to sleep. It's only 0400. I don't know when I'll be back. There's some juice and things for breakfast if you want," McKernan said as he began to dress. The doctor watched him curiously as he put on his clothes, noting the knife and small automatic pistol he strapped to his legs. She hadn't seen them last night when he had undressed, but then her mind had been on other things. She found herself wondering just who this man she found herself attracted to was.

McKernan smiled as he threw a jacket on over his sweater.

Ten minutes later he was in the cross tunnel with Gaeretts. The latter had already taken pictures of the crime scene, and he and Ferris were only waiting for McKernan to get a firsthand look before loading the body on the cart.

"The body was found like this? Not hidden?" McKernan asked. The corpse was laying under a sheet Ferris had draped over it. It was tucked into a pocket against the wall of the tunnel formed by two metal supports.

"Yeah. We haven't moved it. Either our murderer was in a hurry or he's getting sloppy. The body was just pushed up against the wall. Anybody coming through this tunnel would be bound to see it."

"She's just like I found her," Ferris confirmed. "I was doing my rounds coming up Corridor D and I was going to cross over into C. I saw the bag on the floor of the lock. I came through into the cross-tunnel. It was just there tucked back into the shadows between those two stanchions. It would have been pretty hard to miss."

McKernan pulled back the sheet to look at the face.

"Shit!"

"You know her Chief?" Gaeretts asked with his usual sensitivity.

"Yeah. Her name is Mary. She's the witness Ortiz found. I interviewed her yesterday."

"Damn. Ortiz ain't going to be happy," Gaeretts said shaking his head.

"Neither am I. Any idea what happened?"

"Yeah. I think so. It looks like the killer was waiting for her at the airlock in Corridor D. He must have grabbed her when she came through. Ferris found her bag on the floor of the lock. From the marks in the dust he must have dragged her into the tunnel and strangled her. You can see the bruising on the neck. Then he just pushed her into the first dark corner that was handy," Gaeretts recited dispassionately.

"Which way did he go? Did he leave any tracks?"

"Yeah. He went down the tunnel towards C. There's an emergency access lock to the surface near the middle. It looks like he popped up that."

"Great, so he was wearing a surface suit. He must have had this planned."

"It looks like. And he knew the layout of the tunnels. Most people, even out here in the end of Hut Town don't know about the access locks."

"What I want to know is how Buche found out I had talked to Mary so quickly?"

"You think it was him?" Gaeretts asked.

"Yeah."

"Ortiz was checking up on him yesterday afternoon. She contacted the company he works for to see if she could locate him. That must have spooked him."

"Damn."

"It wasn't her fault, Chief. I heard her make the call. She played it cool, just said that she wanted to talk to him as a potential witness to a bar fight. She didn't mention the murders. They said he was out in the middle of nowhere about three hundred kilometers from here on some kind of survey. They said they'd leave a message for him."

"You're sure about him being three hundred kilometers from Mars City?"

"That's what they said."

"OK. Check up on that as soon as you can. If he's still out on a survey, then he's not the killer. And that means we've got somebody else running around strangling people."

"Great. I'll check as soon as we get the body to the hospital. Is there anything else you want us to do here, or can we wrap up and move the body."

"Yeah, if you got pictures, go ahead. If he was wearing a surface suit, I doubt if there are any prints or anything. I'll give the tunnel and lock a sweep to see if I can find anything. Do you need a hand with the cart?"

"No. Ferris and I can manage. We've been getting lots of practice lately," Gaeretts said with a hollow laugh.

After they had left, McKernan walked the length of the tunnel using his flashlight to illuminate the shadows. He didn't find anything more than a few tracks in the dust. He checked out the lock to Corridor D, as well. In the dust on the floor he found a clear print of the boot of a surface suit. The boot showed a lot of use. The person wearing the boot had stood against the wall next to the lock where he wouldn't have been seen by anyone coming in from the corridor. He'd been waiting in ambush.

It was nearly 0600 when McKernan gave up his search. He was wondering whether Beth would still be waiting for him in his bed when his comm buzzed.

"Chief?" came Gaeretts voice when he answered. "You're not going to believe this."

"What is it?" McKernan said with a touch of annoyance.

"We just got a call from Buche's employer. He's gone missing on them. He waited until his partner was out of the Mars Buggy, and then just drove off leaving his buddy stranded with only his surface suit. This was about fourteen hours ago. The stranded guy's suit radio didn't have enough power to reach a satellite so he had to hike five kilo's up a rise until he was in sight of a relay tower. It took six more hours after that for another survey team to reach him. They got to him just before his air and batteries were out. He was one cold, scared puppy by the time they got to him."

"What about Buche. Were they able to track the transponder on the Mars Buggy?"

"Right after this happened the transponder went silent. No clue where he is."

"I think we have a good idea," McKernan said bitterly. "Buche has a lot of experience. He could have driven the three hundred kilometers to Mars City in six or seven hours. That would put him in Hut Town in plenty of time to do the murder."

"Yeah. He probably parked the buggy someplace close but where it would be hard to spot and walked his way in. Probably got in the same way he got out."

"That would be my guess. Try to get some satellite images and see if you can spot the buggy. Though Buche probably has it hidden pretty well. He seems to be a step or two ahead of us."

"You coming in, Chief?" Gaeretts asked.

"I'm going home to get some breakfast first. I'll be to the station by 0900."

Beth was still in his bed when McKernan got back to his hut. He undressed, trying to be as quiet as possible. When he slipped beneath the covers she just pressed up against him without waking.

CHAPTER 27: RECRIMINATIONS AND REGRETS

McKernan tried to take comfort in the warmth of the doctor's body pressed against him, but, finding no rest, he rose and dressed again. To occupy his body, if not his mind he began frying the last of his bacon and a few precious eggs. With a wry smile he thought it was the least he could do to atone for abandoning the doctor in the middle of the night.

While he was still preparing breakfast, Beth appeared from the bedroom. She had pulled one of his sweaters on over her scrubs. The air in the hut was chilly as McKernan, to conserve energy, kept the hut's temperature low in the mornings when he rarely lingered. Even in her disheveled state, and with her hair uncombed, the doctor was still an appealing sight. McKernan regretted that he couldn't stay with her.

"Am I still dreaming? I smell bacon and eggs," then noticing the grim expression on his face she asked, "What's happened?"

"Another body was found. She'd just been killed a few hours earlier."

"Buche?"

"I think so. He's gone missing from his job."

He dished up the eggs and bacon and placed them on the table, followed by two cups of coffee.

"Do you want to talk about it?" Beth asked.

"Not particularly," McKernan said with a sigh. "Sorry. I knew the woman killed. It was Mary, the witness that told us about Buche. The one whose interview I played for you."

"And you think that she was killed because she talked to you?"

McKernan hesitated. "Yes. That's what I think. Somehow, Buche found out about it, and now he's trying to cover his tracks. Or get revenge. Or something. I don't know. All I know is that there's a homicidal maniac roaming Hut Town and I've got to find him before anyone else dies."

"You will, Erik," the doctor said.

"I hope so."

McKernan didn't feel like eating, but he knew better than to waste good food, so he finished his breakfast in silence.

"I'm sorry to rush off like this, but I've got to go," he said when he was done.

"I understand emergencies, Erik. I'm a doctor. You've got a job to do."

"I can walk you to the hospital," McKernan said.

"I was hoping to use your shower," the doctor said sheepishly.

"Sure. No problem," a smile breaking McKernan's face for the first time.

"I was hoping you'd say that," the doctor responded.

"Just be careful when you leave. Go straight down Corridor B to the city. There should be enough people around this hour of the morning that you'll be safe."

"You think Buche might still be out there looking to kill again?"

"At this point I don't know what he'll do. All I know is that he seems to know the ins and outs of Hut Town as well as I do, and that worries me."

"I'll be careful."

"You should be ok once you're out of Hut Town. Look, I've got to go. Enjoy the shower. Lock the hatch when you leave."

"I will. To both."

Gaeretts was waiting at the station when McKernan got there. So was Ortiz. She looked depressed. It was the first time that McKernan could remember seeing her when she didn't seem upbeat.

The first words out of McKernan's mouth was "Any luck with the satellite image?"

"Nothing yet, but there should be an imaging satellite overhead in about thirty minutes. I've scheduled a sweep of the area at its highest resolution."

"Good. Where's Ferris?"

"He's patrolling the far ends of corridors B through D. He also is tying pieces of string on all the external hatches and locks he passes so we can detect if any of them have been used. His idea," Gaeretts said with a touch of pride.

"Good idea. Call everybody in. We're going to need all the help we can get until we catch Buche. How many can we muster."

"Three. Ferris, Kaminski, and Shorter. Four, if Ortiz mans the comms and I go out on patrol. We can make it five if we call in Chen. He's patrolling the road between here and Junction One. He's only fifty kilometers out and can be here in an hour. Miller is patrolling the East road, but he's more than a day's travel away. Everybody else is out at one of the camps or in the boonies."

"Bring in Chen," McKernan said, then paused. "No, instead, have him drive a circuit from around the end of Hut Town to five kilometers out and see if he can spot Buche's buggy. If he can't turn anything up in a couple of hours have him drive the spaces between the corridors. We know that Buche used the hatch on the cross-tunnel between C and D. Maybe Chen can find his tracks."

"It's pretty hard packed around Hut Town. Too much traffic for too many years."

"I know, but maybe we'll get lucky," McKernan shrugged.

"What should we tell people out in Hut Town?" Gaeretts asked.

"I don't want to start a panic. But we've got to tell people to be careful. At this point we can't be sure who Buche might go after. Just tell people we're looking for a fugitive who might be dangerous. Show his picture around so they know who he is and tell them to contact the station if they see him."

"Right, Chief. One more thing. Greenwood was at the hospital when we brought the body in," Gaeretts mentioned as an aside. "He took a quick look. He said to tell you that the bruising around her neck matched that on Lola's. He's pretty sure both were killed by the same man."

"Not really new information," McKernan spat. Then more steadily, "Well at least we can be fairly certain that we only have one killer on the loose."

"Anything else, Chief?"

"When Kaminski and Shorter get here, assign each one a corridor. Ferris can take C. You can work the cross tunnels. I'd like to have them work in pairs, but we just don't have enough manpower. Make sure everyone keeps in touch. And tell them not to hesitate to shoot if they spot Buche. He's strong as an ox and probably can take any one of them in a hand to hand fight."

McKernan retired to his office. Not for the first time he cursed the bureaucratic short-sightedness of the Trust Authority which gave him only a handful of constables with which to police a planet. Half of his force was scattered at remote camps and mining operations around Mars and a quarter of it were needed to patrol the five thousand kilometers of road that stretched to the east and west of Mars City. He had had to pull one constable from the city force to substitute for Ortiz while she was on maternity leave, and he had another constable on medical leave recovering from a broken arm suffered in breaking up a late night bar fight.

"Sir?" It was Ortiz at his doorway. She looked like hell.

"What is it, Ortiz?"

"It's my fault, isn't it? That Mary is dead?"

McKernan looked at the constable. Ortiz was a good cop. Smart, dedicated, good with people. But she had never had to face a situation like this before. He could sense that she was in a fragile state. The fact that she was eight months pregnant wasn't helping things.

"It wasn't your fault, Elena," McKernan said. He wasn't sure if he had ever addressed her by her first name before. "You couldn't have known."

"But I was the one that let Buche onto the fact that we were looking for him."

"Gaeretts said that you just said you wanted to talk to him as a potential witness about a fight. You didn't mention anything about the killings, did you?

"No," Ortiz replied hesitatingly.

"And you never mentioned Mary's name."

"No."

"And Buche at the time was three hundred kilometers away. You couldn't have known that he would dump his partner and drive to Hut Town and find out that Mary had talked to you, and do it all in the space of ten or twelve hours."

"But I keep thinking that I could have done something different."

"What could you have done that would have changed anything? We don't really have the facilities to put someone in protective custody and we certainly don't have the manpower to have given her a bodyguard. Especially when we didn't have any idea that Buche was anywhere close to Hut Town."

"I know that, sir. But it doesn't make any difference."

"Look, Elena. You're a good cop. One of the best I've got. But even good cops get put in situations where they can't win. This is one of them. But because of your good work we at least know who the killer is. We'll get him. It's only a matter of time."

"But how could he have found out about Mary, sir?" Ortiz asked plaintively. "I was very discrete about talking to her. How could Buche have found out so quickly?"

"That's been bothering me, too, Constable. Buche ditched his partner at 1600 as far as we can tell. Even driving flat out, he couldn't have gotten to Hut Town much earlier than 2200. We think he parked his buggy some distance away so that it wouldn't be spotted and walked in. That probably took another hour. Yet Mary was murdered no later than about 0200. Probably earlier. And she was ambushed. Buche was waiting for her. Probably had been for some time. That really didn't leave him much time to go around asking questions. It's almost as if he knew ahead of time what he was going to do. Knew that Mary had talked before you made that call."

"Do you really think that. Sir?" Ortiz asked.

"I don't know. It makes as much sense as anything. Look, I'm short-handed as it is. I need you to keep it together, Constable. Do you think you can do that? If not, let me know. Under the circumstances I'll understand."

"No, sir. I'm alright."

"Good."

At that moment Gaeretts poked his head into the office. "The satellite images just came in. I've put them up on the big screen in the bullpen."

"Let's go see if we can spot Buche's buggy, Constable," McKernan said.

They spent the next few minutes panning back and forth through the images of Hut Town but with no luck.

"I never realized how much junk is just lying around out there," Gaeretts said in disgust.

"They've been dumping things since the first mission. The only thing that keeps it halfway in check are the scavengers," McKernan commented.

"Buche is a smart one. He could have done something clever like parked the vehicle in one of the vehicle parks. Who'd notice one more buggy?"

"I don't think so," McKernan said. "Most of those are to the west by the spaceport or over to the east of the city. He wants access to the far end of Hut Town. My guess is that he's somewhere to the north."

"Well I don't see anything, and these images are good enough to spot a man let alone something as big as a buggy."

"What are these structures," McKernan asked pointing to a scattering of buildings.

"Most of them are old equipment shelters. They're basically just arched roofs with open ends."

"Big enough to hide a buggy?"

"That's what they were made for," Gaeretts agreed.

"Have Chen start checking them out when he gets here."

"There must be dozens of them. Maybe hundreds."

"Then the sooner he gets started the better," McKernan said. "Have him download this image so he knows where to look."

Chapter 28: Discoveries and Revelations

For the moment, there was nothing to do but play a waiting game. Ferris, Kaminski, and Shorter were patrolling the corridors. Gaeretts left to join them after they had finished looking at the satellite images. Chen was still an hour out, driving in from road patrol. McKernan's instincts were to join the constables, but he knew it wasn't the time to follow his instincts. It was better to wait at the station until some sign of Buche surfaced, then join the hunt.

He had to admit, too, that he wasn't sure about Ortiz's state of mind. Mary's death bothered her. It bothered him. She had put her trust in them, and they had failed her. He didn't think that Ortiz would break down, but she might do something rash, and he already had enough to regret about how this case had been handled.

"Ortiz, now that Gaeretts is out in Hut Town, you're handling communications. I want you to keep track of where everybody is at all times. I want them to check in before they enter every new section of corridor, every time they are about to go through a lock. And let me know if anyone is late in checking in."

He hoped that handling the comm. would keep her mind busy. He only wished he had something to keep his own occupied while they waited. He went into his office and brought up Buche's file, but nothing new grabbed his attention.

The minutes crept by. Out in the outer office he could hear Ortiz on the comm as each of the patrollers checked in in turn, each with nothing to report. If Buche was in Hut Town he'd gone to ground. There were plenty of places to hide out at the ends of the corridors; unused or derelict buildings, seldom used air locks, service tunnels. There were even more places for a man to hide if he was willing to go outside and breathe suit air for a while. Since coming to Mars Buche had probably spent half his time in a suit. A few hours on the surface wouldn't faze him in the least.

McKernan wondered if it would be worthwhile to request another set of satellite images. He decided it was. They just might get lucky and spot Buche. Unfortunately when he asked he was told that a satellite wouldn't be in position for another three hours. He asked for it anyway.

At 1005 Chen reported in. He had reached the outskirts of Mars City and wanted instructions.

"I want you to check all of the old shelters and unused buildings off the end of Hut Town. We think that Buche may have parked his buggy in one of them."

"That's what Gaeretts said. He sent me a set of images. I've got a map of the area, too, but who knows what it includes."

"We think he walked in last night from wherever he parked the buggy and entered Hut Town through a service lock in the outermost cross-tunnel between C and D Corridors. I doubt that he would have chosen to walk in more than five kilometers. Why don't you start at that distance and work your way in checking every likely hiding place within a five click radius of the end of Corridor C. Keep in touch with Ortiz so she can check off each location as you verify they're clean."

"Roger that, sir. I'm on my way. I should be at the first possibility in ten minutes."

"Good," McKernan said, as he hung up the comm.

"Sir?" Ortiz said to get his attention.

"Have they found something?"

"No, sir. But I think I might have something else. I did a back check on communications with Buche. Out where he was, ordinary cell phone coverage wouldn't work. Everything would have had to have been relayed through either a satellite or one of the relay towers. That makes it a lot easier to track. Anyway, Buche had a call relayed to him yesterday at 1217. It was from a Seth Padgett in Hut Town."

"Do we know who this Seth Padgett is?" McKernan asked.

"He works as a bartender and bouncer at Thelma's. I checked his personnel file. He's a Canadian from Edmonton. But he worked as a rigger up in the Arctic same time that Buche was there."

"You think they know each other?"

"Padgett called him, didn't he, sir?" Ortiz asked, sounding smug.

"Do you recognize Padgett's picture?"

"No, but that doesn't mean he didn't hear me asking questions. Or hear that I was asking them."

"But you didn't know about Buche then, did you?"

"No. I didn't find out about him until I talked to Mary. But I was asking about Mabel Johnson. If Buche was the one who beat Mabel up and this Padgett knew about it he might have wanted to warn Buche."

"I think that it's worth looking into. Have Gaeretts bring Padgett in. Good work, Constable."

Padgett, when Gaeretts dragged him into the station, proved to be a thin man in his middle thirties. He looked like he had more than a little native American, or what the Canadians like to call first nation, blood in him. His clothes were disheveled, and not just from Gaeretts' efforts in bringing him in. He sat in the tiny cubicle they used for interrogations with a sullen expression on his face.

According to his file, he had come out to Mars to work construction, same as Buche, but after a couple of years had lost his job because he drank too much. Rather than take advantage of the return fare that was a condition of every employment contract on Mars, he had stuck around, taking the bartender job at Thelma's, the largest and most notorious of the saloons catering to miners in town on a spree.

"What am I here for?" he asked when McKernan sat down across the small table from him. Gaeretts still stood, just behind and a little to the side of Padgett's seat.

"Do you know a Pierre Buche?" McKernan asked coldly.

"I don't know. Maybe. You meet a lot of guys in my line of work. I don't usually bother with names." His attitude was belligerent though he looked less certain of his position than he sounded.

"You placed a call to him yesterday."

"Oh. Pierre. Yeah, I know him. We used to work on the same job up in Canada."

"What did you call him about?" McKernan asked. "I bet it wasn't just to reminisce about old times. Or to talk about hockey, either."

"It's none of your business."

"It's my business if it involves murder," McKernan said. "We found the body of a woman named Mary last night. If you had anything to do with that you could be considered an accessory."

"I didn't have anything to do with any murder, and you can't prove it."

"Maybe not, but I can see you're sent back to Earth as an undesirable. I'll let them consider whether to prosecute or not."

"You can't do that."

"I can send anyone I like back to Earth if I feel their presence is detrimental to the public order. Let's face it, Padgett, you've got no one to back you up. No one cares whether you get shipped back or not. It's not like you still work for one of the companies. I bet even your boss at Thelma's wouldn't lift a finger for you. All I have to do is say the word."

McKernan could tell that Padgett was getting nervous. His eyes flickered from side to side and he licked his lips repeatedly.

"OK. I don't know nothing about no murder, understand. But I did call Pierre yesterday."

"Why did you call him?" McKernan asked again.

"One of your constables, at least I think she was a constable, though it looked like she was going to pop a kid at any moment. Anyway, I overheard her asking around about Mabel Johnson. I knew her as Lola. Well, about four months ago Buche knocked her around a little bit. Not sure why. He's gotten a little crazy the last few years. He's got a thing about women with dyed hair. Seems he knocked this Lola woman around. I thought maybe he'd get in trouble about it, so I gave him a call warning him and telling him to keep a low profile. That's all, I swear."

"You know Lola is dead, too, don't you?" McKernan asked casually.

"No. Christ. I just knew I hadn't seen her around lately. But she was always talking about how she was going back to Earth with the money she made. I just figured she finally did it."

"What else did you tell Buche? Did you mention anything about Mary?"

"I don't know anyone named Mary. I swear. I just told Buche that questions were being asked."

"You're sure that's all?"

Padgett looked like he was thinking for a moment. It seemed to take an effort on his part. "I might have mentioned that the cop was talking to this woman with red hair and acting like she was real pleased with what she was hearing. But I didn't know the woman other than I'd seen her around. I didn't know her name or anything."

"Did you describe her to Buche?"

"Yeah, maybe. At least the hair. It was a pretty noticeable color. Look, I'm cooperating. Can I go now?"

"Not just yet," McKernan answered. "Do you know where Buche is now?"

"He's out somewhere doing a survey or something. I had to do a relay to reach him."

"We have reason to believe he's somewhere in Hut Town. Any ideas where he might hole up?"

"He's here? No, I didn't know he was coming here. I told him he should stay away."

"But do you know where he might hide, if he was here?" McKernan repeated.

"Could be anywhere. I do know that he knows the far end of Hut Town better than just about anyone. He's a bit looney on the subject if you know what I mean. He'd spend half his time when he was in on R and R roaming the corridors and checking out empty huts. Always struck me as a waste of time when he could be drinking or whoring."

"Anything else you can tell us?"

"No. I've told you everything. You've got to believe me. I don't know nothing about any murders."

"I think we're done here, Gaeretts. Put Mr. Padgett in the detention cell."

"Hey, what's the deal," Padgett complained. "I cooperated."

"Has it struck you that Buche has already killed one witness?" McKernan asked. "You might be next on his list. Personally, I couldn't care one way or the other, but I'm not going to have any more murders if I can help it. Take him away, sergeant."

As Gaeretts was escorting Padgett to the cells Ortiz popped her head in the door. "Chen's on the comm. He wants to talk to you."

McKernan went to the communications console. "What have you found?"

"Like you said, I found a buggy stashed in one of the old dust shelters. It's about two kilometers off the end of Corridor C. I checked the registration number. It's the one that Buche drove off in. What do you want me to do?"

"Any signs of life?"

"Not that I've seen. I've been staring at it for about five minutes now. Do you want me to go in and check it out?"

"No. Not yet. Buche is dangerous. Wait till I can join you. Find a spot where you can keep it under observation but not too close. Don't do anything unless it looks like Buche might give us the slip."

"Fine by me, Chief. How soon will you be here?"

"It'll take me maybe forty minutes or more to suit up and get out there. I'll walk out from the end of Corridor D. That should keep Buche from spotting me if he's watching."

"I'll be waiting for you."

"Good. McKernan out."

McKernan headed to the locker where he kept his surface suit. Gaeretts followed.

"Do you want me to go with you, Chief?" the sergeant asked.

"No. We don't know for sure that Buche is at the buggy. Chen and I should be able to handle him if he is. I want you to coordinate things while I'm gone."

"Aye-aye, Chief," Gaeretts said. He helped McKernan with the checkout as he put on his surface suit. He nodded approvingly as the Inspector strapped the holster belt of his .44 magnum revolver around his waist. The only one of its kind on Mars, it had a lot more stopping power than the standard issue 5 mm pistols. From the weapons locker he took down a pump action short barreled shotgun. It wasn't much for range or accuracy, but hard to beat against a man in a pressure suit. He left the station with his helmet in one hand and the shotgun in the other.

Chapter 29: Coming Up Empty

McKernan moved through the halls of Mars City at a trot. In the Grand Concourse the few startled onlookers moved to avoid him. The sight of someone in a surface suit was a rare spectacle within the city. The sight of someone in a surface suit carrying a naked gun was even rarer. Most of them knew the Chief Inspector by sight at least, but none could envision why he might be so heavily armed.

He left the concourse and headed out the length of Corridor D. That was probably the least likely for Buche to be in if he was in Hut Town at all. If he was, as McKernan hoped, holed up in the Mars buggy, coming at him from the end of D would probably offer the least risk of being observed.

McKernan fretted as he jogged down the kilometer and a half of corridor, delayed by the locks every hundred meters, down its length. Including the time it had taken him to suit up, over a half hour had passed since Chen's call.

Kaminski was waiting for him at the exit lock at the end of Corridor D. The constable was a reliable man. He'd been on Mars longer than McKernan had. Still, the inspector could tell that he was keyed up with that hyper-alertness some men get in action.

"Sure you don't want to wait until some of us could suit up, Chief?"

"It would take too long," McKernan said declining the suggestion. "Besides, we don't know for sure that Buche is in the buggy. If he is, Chen and I can take care of him."

He set his helmet onto the locking ring of his suit and gave it a twist. As a matter of routine, Kaminski went through the check out procedure. Satisfied, he gave a pat on his helmet and McKernan entered the lock.

Cycling between the pressure of the Hut Town and the surface, the lock took longer than the those between sections of the corridor. McKernan waited patiently, his eye on the readout until he saw that the lock was equalized with the outside. Satisfied, he opened the hatch and stepped out onto the surface of Mars.

It took him a moment to get his bearings. Whereas a moment earlier he had dwelt in the confines of a metal tube only a few meters in diameter, he now could see all the way to the low ridge far off on the horizon. This close to Mars City, it wasn't a barren landscape. On the contrary, it was covered with the works of man. Off to his right he could see the expanse of the solar energy farm, several square kilometers of solar panels that provided a portion Mars City's energy demands. To his left and rear lay the conglomeration of pneumatic architecture known as Hut Town. In front of him was a gently sloping plain criss-crossed with vehicle tracks and interrupted here and there by various structures, some abandoned, some still in use. The focus of Mars City had been moving to the south and west since the construction of the first permanent buildings, but there was still considerable activity north of Hut Town.

Picking his direction by the lay of the Corridor D and his memory of the satellite image, McKernan headed out in the easy lope that is the most efficient pace for a man on foot to cover ground in the low gravity of Mars. Chen's buggy should be a little more than a kilometer and a half, just over a mile, ahead of him.

Chen was waiting for him outside his buggy fifteen minutes later when McKernan arrived. The inspector noted with approval that the constable was carrying a short barreled carbine in addition to the pistol strapped to his waist.

"The buggy is right over there," Chen said, pointing to a half buried dust shelter some five hundred meters to the northeast of where they stood. The shelter consisted of a half cylinder of light metal open at each end, and just big enough to drive a Mars buggy into. There wasn't much in the way of cover, but if Buche was inside the buggy, they could avoid observation by keeping the side of the shelter between them and the buggy. If Buche was outside, there was no way that he wouldn't be able to spot them. McKernan wasn't sure that it mattered. As far as he knew, Buche didn't have any firearms. Guns were strictly regulated and relatively scarce on Mars. He would probably have a knife, though, and there were a number of common tools that could become deadly weapons in a hand to hand fight.

The two of them started towards the shelter, moving slower than McKernan had on his jog out from Hut Town. As they approached the shelter ten minutes later they held their weapons at the ready. Fortunately there had been no sign of Buche.

For a moment they paused just outside the shelter, standing along the side where they couldn't be seen from the buggy inside. The shelter was about fifteen meters long, just a few meters longer than the buggy.

"What now?" Chen asked.

"You go to that end, I'll go to this one. When I give the sign, poke your head around and see if you can spot Buche. Ready?"

McKernan waited until Chen was in position, then gave a hand sign, simultaneously popping his head around the edge of the shelter. Anticlimactically, there was no sign of Buche. Only the buggy sitting in the middle.

Cautiously, they moved to the side of the buggy, trying to stay out of the line of sight from the large windshield at the front. The buggy stood high on its large tires. The bottom of the front window was just less than the height of a man above the ground. McKernan was the taller of the two. He stepped around to the front of the buggy and tried to peer inside, while Chen kept a watch on the airlock on the vehicle's side. The light wasn't good, but as far as he could tell, the buggy was empty.

"I don't see him," McKernan said.

"So what now?" Chen asked. McKernan knew what he was thinking. The interior of a buggy wasn't that big and there weren't many places to hide. But there were a few; the inside of the lock itself, the toilet compartment, a couple of storage lockers.

McKernan checked the readout on the side lock. It showed that the pressure in the lock was at Mars normal. That indicated that the last person to use the lock had exited. The chances were good that Buche was not in the buggy. Their options were limited. The lock would only hold one person at a time, so whoever entered the buggy would do so alone.

"OK. I open the lock and step in. You move around to the front to cover me. I'll cycle through and check inside."

"You're the boss, Chief," Chen replied cheerfully.

McKernan opened the hatch of the lock. It was, as he had hoped and expected, empty. He stepped up into the lock and closed the hatch. The inner hatch had a small window in it, but it didn't provide much of a view of the inside of the buggy. Shrugging, McKernan pressed the control to cycle the lock. He could feel the pressure building through his suit. Almost as an aside, he noticed that his revolver was gripped in his hand.

The indicator on the lock showed that the pressure was equalized with the inside of the vehicle. He worked the handle, pushing the hatch open a crack so he could see towards the driver's seat. There was no one there. He opened the hatch all the way and stepped through. It only took a moment to confirm that the buggy was empty. He gave a thumbs up to Chen who had been waiting at the front.

McKernan waited while the lock cycled again to let Chen in. He gave a quick examination to the interior of the buggy, but there was nothing that was out of place. All the equipment seemed to be stowed in its proper place. That wasn't surprising. People who lived for weeks at a time in such tight quarters tended to be neat.

"So what now? Do we sit here and wait for him to come back?"

"No," McKernan answered. "He's probably somewhere in Hut Town. He's probably got something planned. I just don't know what. We've got to flush him out before then. But I don't want to take a chance on him giving us the slip. I'll go back inside and organize a drive. If he sees enough of us coming after him, maybe he'll bolt. I'd just as soon try to take him down outside. There's less chance of an innocent bystander getting hurt. I want you to go back to your buggy and take up a position where you can watch the buggy here and the end of Corridor C. If you spot him, take him down."

"Any way I can?"

"Any way you can. He's already killed three people."

CHAPTER 30: WHERE'S ORTIZ?

McKernan left Chen in a position a little less than a kilometer off the end of Corridor C. From there he would have a good chance of spotting anyone exiting Hut Town and heading for where Buche had parked his buggy.

From there it took him ten minutes to covered the distance to the airlock. Once he had cycled through into the corridor he contacted the office to check on the status of the search. The voice on the comm wasn't Ortiz's.

"Who is this?"

"Cox, sir?" came the reply. Cox was the constable who was off duty with a broken arm.

"What are you doing there and where is Ortiz?" McKernan asked with more than a little annoyance.

"When I heard that you had called in everybody, I came in to see if there was any way I could help. Ortiz asked me to take over manning communications. She said there was something she had to do. I said sure, I can manage that one-handed."

"Did she say where she was going?"

"No. She just explained things to me and took off. Did I do something wrong, sir?" It was dawning on Cox that he might be in trouble.

"It's not your fault, Cox. It just that we've got a homicidal maniac on the loose and I was trying to keep Ortiz out of the way. You're sure she didn't say anything about what she was up to?"

"No, sir."

"If she checks in, or shows up back at the station, tell her to stay there. She's not to leave until I give the order. Got that?"

"Yes, sir."

"Has anyone reported any sign of Buche?"

"No, sir."

"OK. Have everybody meet me at Lock 3 Corridor C in fifteen minutes. And tell them that if they see Ortiz they should tell her to get back to the station immediately."

"Yes, sir," Cox answered.

"Good. McKernan out."

The next thing McKernan did was to call Dr. Haestert.

"Hello, Beth. You haven't seen Ortiz, have you?"

"Elena? No, why?"

"She's gone missing. We're pretty sure Buche is hiding out somewhere at the far end of Hut Town. I was hoping Ortiz had an appointment with you, but I'm afraid that she may be trying to track down Buche on her own."

"She's not scheduled for another appointment for a few days yet, Erik, and she hasn't come in on her own. Sorry."

"That's what I was afraid of. If you do see her, don't let her out of your sight."

"Will do. And Erik—"

"Yes."

"I hate to bother you with this, but Elena could be going into labor any time now. We just haven't had much experience with pregnancies under Martian gravity."

"Oh, great," McKernan sighed. "It's not bad enough I've got a maniac on the loose. Look, Beth, I'll let you know as soon as I hear anything about Ortiz. You might also want to get the emergency room ready just in case, too."

"I will. Take care Erik."

Gaeretts and the other three were waiting for him when he reached Lock 3. The first thing he did was ask any of them if they had seen Ortiz. Shorter said that she had gone by him heading out D. He had asked her what she was doing and she said she was checking on something and that "McKernan would understand."

"What's that about, Chief?" Gaeretts asked.

"You've got me. You notice she didn't say I would approve."

"So what do you want us to do?" the sergeant asked.

"Our best chance to get Buche is to drive him out into the open, and the way to do that is to start from one end of Hut Town and push to the other, checking every possible hiding place along the way. We'll move in unison so that he doesn't have a chance to work his way behind us. Kaminski, Ferris, Shorter, you'll each take a corridor as before. Gaeretts and I will work the cross tunnels. Knock on the hatch of every hut you pass and make sure that Buche isn't hiding inside. Tell anyone you see to get inside and stay there till we give the all clear."

"What if a hatch is locked?" Ferris asked.

"If it's locked, Buche probably couldn't get inside, but mark it anyway. If we get to the end of Hut Town and we haven't found him, then we'll come back and check anyplace we couldn't get into on the first sweep. Oh, and if you do meet anyone, flash Buche's picture and see if they've seen him."

"What about the utility space underneath the corridors?" Gaeretts asked. "That's where we found the first body."

"You and I will check those while the rest are checking the huts in each length of corridor. And remember, we don't move onto the next section until we checked everything in all three corridors."

"What about A and E?"

"We don't have enough men to cover all five corridors. Those two are shorter and there are more people moving around. As far as we know Buche has avoided them. At least that's what I'm hoping. Any other questions?—No? Then let's get moving. One other thing. Cox, are you there?" McKernan said into his comm.

"I'm here, sir."

"Good. I want everyone conferenced in on an open channel at all times. Got that?"

"I'm switching it in now, sir."

"Everybody live?"

Their voices echoed through the multiple comms as they checked in.

"OK, let's move."

They moved through into the airlock, Kaminski and Gaeretts heading through the left cross tunnel into B, McKernan and Shorter right into D.

Nothing turned up in the first section they checked. It was mostly residential, the owners at work and the hatches locked. At the few huts that had businesses operating in them, the response was negative. No one had seen Buche. No one had seen Ortiz, either. The cross-tunnels and service spaces were empty, too.

The next two sections produced the same results. The residents who were home hadn't seen anything. Hadn't even been aware that a manhunt was going on. McKernan fretted that it was taking too long to search each length of corridor, but to speed things up would risk missing something. Still, at this rate it would be after midnight before they reached the far end of Hut Town.

As they worked their way farther along the corridors, the spaces got shabbier. The prime locations for residences and businesses were all at the Mars City end of the corridors. By the time they were nearly a kilometer out along the corridors they began to run into huts that were unoccupied or derelict. Some didn't even hold pressure, anymore, waiting for the day when someone would fix them up again and move in. Despite whatever the Trust Authority might claim, property rights in Hut Town had always been fluid and ad hoc in nature.

The residences and businesses of the more prosperous end of Hut Town were giving way to the flops, dive bars and bordellos catering to miners. But as they moved into these, their task actually became easier. There were more people around, and while normally they wouldn't give the time of day to a constable, there was something in the look of determination in the faces of McKernan and his men that made them more responsive. The deaths of first Lola and then Mary had made people nervous. If the police could take care of it so much the better.

They were on the next to last section of corridor when Kaminski checked in.

"What you got, Kaminski?"

"There's a guy here who runs a noodle cart. He says he saw a big guy in a surface suit dragging a 'pregnant lady' down the corridor. I showed him the picture of Buche. He says he's not sure, but it could be him. He's not sure about the woman. He didn't get a good look."

"Did Buche have his helmet with him?"

"Just a second, I'll ask," Kaminski said. "He's not sure, but he doesn't think so."

"Did he see where he went?"

"He said they went through the lock at the end of the section. And he said that the pregnant lady wasn't wearing a surface suit."

"OK. I want you to finish up that section of corridor and move into the airlock and stay there until Gaeretts and I can get there. Ferris, Shorter. Finish up with corridors C and D. Let me know when you're done."

McKernan was in C corridor, Gaeretts in D. They had both been checking the service tunnels underneath. "Gaeretts, I'll meet you at the airlock for the cross tunnel between C and D. We'll go through the tunnel to B together. Got that?"

"Right, Chief."

"Let's move."

Chapter 31: Tightening the Noose

McKernan and Gaeretts made their way through the cross tunnel between corridors C and B, shining their flashes into every dark corner and shadowy crevice hoping that the beams of light would reveal nothing. Fortunately, the result of their search was negative. If the vendor had indeed spotted Buche, he had headed into the last section of corridor B and not made his way across to C or D. Hopefully, it also meant that he still had Ortiz with him and she was still alive.

Kaminski was waiting for them in the airlock. This was a three-way affair, with hatches to the last two sections of Corridor B as well as the cross-tunnel to C. There was no cross-tunnel to A as it did not extend out this far. Buche was trapped somewhere on the other side of the hatch in the last section of the corridor.

Instinctively, McKernan glanced at the pressure gauge set into the control panel next to the hatch. The pressure on the other side of the hatch was even lower than that in most of the corridors, just barely enough to be breathable.

"What's in this section?" the inspector asked.

"Not much," replied Gaeretts. "This far out was mostly storage and repair facilities. Larger model huts. That's all been abandoned. Some of the contractors still use them for temporary warehouse space when they have materials they don't want to leave on the surface. Might be some other people stashing stuff they don't want other people to know about." A certain percentage of Hut Town's economy was based on recycling salvaged material. As long as it was really abandoned, the practice was tolerated, even encouraged. That didn't mean that the scavengers didn't occasionally scavenge from each other.

"No residents?"

"Not officially. Too far out. Might be some squatters, but they'd have to be pretty desperate."

"That's a break, then," McKernan said. "We won't have to worry about bystanders."

There was a small window set in the airlock hatch. McKernan put his eye to it but there was nothing to see. There were no lights on in the corridor.

"Someone's turned off the lights," he grunted.

"Or stolen the fixtures," Kaminski commented. "We're lucky the corridor still holds air."

"What's the plan?" Gaeretts asked.

"We equalize the pressure in the lock. You and I will go through. Kaminski, I want you to stay in the lock and cover us until we make sure Buche isn't waiting in the corridor. Then we search the huts until we find them. Got your weapons and flashes ready?"

Both of the men gave their assent.

"Let's turn off the light in here before I open the hatch. No sense making ourselves easy targets."

Gaeretts fumbled with the fixture. There wasn't any on-off switch. Finally he gave up and just yanked the bulb out of its connector. The sound of it skittering away on the deck of the lock echoed through the chamber. The only illumination left was the faint glow of the read-outs on the lock controls.

McKernan pressed the button that equalized pressure with the next section. There was a brief moment of the hissing of escaping gas until the lock was at the same pressure as the corridor on the other side. He undogged the hatch and gave it a gentle push.

Slowly the hatch swung outward into the corridor. He paused a moment, listening for sounds from the darkness, but there was nothing to hear. Satisfied, he stepped through, moving to the right. Behind him, he could hear Gaeretts following, the sergeant moving to the left side of the corridor.

The darkness in the length of corridor wasn't quite total. The overheads were out, but the faint red glow of LED read-outs marked some of the hatches leading into the huts on either side.

Cautiously, McKernan raised the flash in his left hand up and away from his body. He held his gun at the ready in his right. He flicked the switch on the flash and a thin beam flared out a few meters into the darkness. Gaeretts' flash did the same to his left. There was no way the flashes could penetrate the hundred meter length of the corridor.

"I want to make sure the corridor is clear before we begin to check the huts," McKernan said. The two men began the long walk to the far end. As they moved along, McKernan kept his flash pointing straight ahead while Gaeretts' probed the sides of the corridor.

Not only was the air in the corridor thin, it was cold, scarcely above freezing. McKernan, still in his surface suit, was glad for the warmth it provided. Gaeretts, though dressed in a heavy sweater, wasn't so lucky. Occasionally their condensing breath would form a cloud where the beam of one of the flashes caught it.

When they had reached the end of the corridor McKernan called out the all clear to Kaminski. A moment later, a thin beam of light shown through the hatch. Kaminski had restored the bulb to its place in the airlock fixture. It provided just enough light to illuminate the first twenty meters.

"Any way to get the lights on in here," McKernan asked.

In response, Gaeretts pointed his flash at the nearest overhead fixture. The bulb was gone.

"They're all like that. Somebody has stripped this section clear. Maybe Buche, maybe just scavengers."

"Maybe Entwhistle's men trying to find replacements for other corridors," McKernan commented.

"Probably," Gaeretts grunted. "So what now?"

"Did you see any tracks pointing to a specific hatch?"

"No. There's been enough recent activity in here to have stirred up the dust so you can't tell. The lock's been used recently, too. Someone coming in, not out," he said pointing at the pressure readout. It showed that the lock was at the same pressure as the corridor.

"Let's start at the other end and work our way out."

"You're the boss, Chief," Gaeretts responded.

When they got to the end of the section McKernan said, "Kaminski, you keep an eye on the corridor. Gaeretts and I will check out the huts."

He undogged the first hatch on the right and swung it open, keeping his body shielded by wall. The lock was empty. Stepping into the lock chamber, he undid the dogs holding the inner hatch and swung it open. The space echoed hollowly. Gaeretts shown the beam of his flash into the hut. It was empty. Had been for a long time. The dust lay heavy on the floor. There were no signs of footprints. By the signs, no one had been in that hut for years.

They repeated the procedure with the first hatch on the left. The beam of Gaeretts flash revealed a stack of metal girders piled in the center of the hut. McKernan noticed that they had been chained together. Footprints marred the dust. Lots of footprints.

The hut was a big one. Fifty meters long, twenty wide. They checked its length, moving cautiously until they reached the far end. All they found were stacks of beams, pipes, and other construction material. The far end of the hut had a big airlock, nearly ten meters in length. That explained the construction material. This was probably one of the few huts that had a lock big enough to bring things in from the surface. There was no sign of Buche.

The next hut on the right was empty. So was the next on the left. The third on the right had had a hasp welded to it and a very impressive looking padlock. Whatever was inside, it wasn't Buche, but it aroused McKernan's curiosity. Gaeretts just shrugged.

McKernan was just about to open the inner hatch of the airlock on the next hut when Gaeretts caught his hand. He pointed at the read-out. There was no air on the other side. The hut was a derelict at surface pressure.

Ferris's voice sounded on their communicator. "We've checked the last sections of C and D, sir. What do you want us to do?"

"You might as well join us in B," McKernan answered.

"Do we wait for them?" Gaeretts asked.

"No. We might as well keep checking."

They had worked their way about half-way down the corridor. Only six more hatches remained.

McKernan opened the next hatch. Before he could step into the lock Gaerretts pointed to the dust on the floor. There was the clear impression in the dust of a pair of boots being dragged. Small boots.

Chapter 32: Siege

"Ortiz?"

"I think we have to operate on that assumption," McKernan answered tersely.

"How do you want to play it?" Gaeretts asked.

"Carefully. I think we need to think this through. Let's move back into the corridor." He stepped back outside, gently shutting the outer hatch behind them.

"OK. Let's say Buche is in there with Ortiz. He probably doesn't know that we're out here. We know he was wearing a surface suit but not a helmet when he was last seen. There's a good chance his helmet was stashed in the hut here, but we also know that Ortiz wasn't wearing a surface suit. That's going to affect how Buche acts. What do we know about the hut on the other side of the hatch?"

"I'm not sure," Gaeretts said. "I've never been inside any of the huts in this section before today. No reason."

"Me neither," McKernan said. "Cox, you there?"

"I'm here, Chief. What do you need?"

"I want you to look up a hut in the database. Third from the end on the left side looking out. I want a physical description of the layout, contents, anything that might help us. Buche is holed up inside with Ortiz. I need to know what I'm going to find on the other side of the hatch."

"Gotcha. Give me a second," Cox replied. They could hear the clicking of his keyboard through the comm.

"Cox, we got some satellite images earlier. You might take a look at those, too. It should show the end of B Corridor."

"Right. I've got a description of the hut. It's a long one, sixty-five meters long, ten wide. The file says it was originally used for growing plants. When all that was moved to the Farm it was used for storage. It's currently listed as unoccupied. I'm bringing up the blueprints now. Got 'em. Don't know how useful they are. They're the originals. They show racks of plant trays running down both sides of the hut. My guess is they pulled all of that stuff out when they consolidated all the agriculture after they built the Farm. No telling what they put in its place, and that was years ago. It's probably been scavenged since."

The latter was a sure bet. Martians were great believers in recycling. Anything useful had probably been taken not long after it was abandoned, whether officially or not.

"Do the blueprints show any partitions, anything structural?"

"Yeah. There are bulkheads in place at twenty and forty meters. There's also a partition at the far end. It looks like an office or storage on one side and a head on the other. There's an airlock at the far end. Actually two locks, one for cargo and a smaller one for personnel."

"Anything else that might be useful?"

"Sorry, Chief. That's all I've been able to dig up. I'll keep looking, though."

"Thanks. I want you to contact Chen. Tell him to drive around to the end of the hut. Tell me when he's in place."

"Roger, Chief."

"So what do we do now?" Gaeretts asked.

"We wait until Chen is in position. I'm the only one wearing a surface suit, and I left my helmet at the exit lock in C Corridor. It would take too long to fetch it."

Cox broke in on the comm., "Chen says that he should be in place in five minutes."

"Good. Keep us informed."

"There's something else you should know."

"What is it?"

"On a hunch, I checked if Ortiz had received any calls on her phone right before she left, and she did. It was from a woman named Dolores. It was recorded. I played it back. Hope that was all right?"

"Don't worry about it. What was it about."

"This Dolores, who I take it is a working girl, calls Ortiz and says she knows where Buche is, but she doesn't want to say over the phone on account of what happened to Mary. Asks Ortiz to meet her at a place in Corridor B. Does that make sense."

"Unfortunately, yes. Though Ortiz should have known better. Mary was the most recent victim and the one who told us about Buche. Good work, Cox."

"Must have been a trap," Gaeretts said.

"More like an ambush. Buche probably got this Dolores to lure Ortiz to a meeting. Probably someplace Ortiz would think safe, then he ambushed her on the way."

"So, are we dealing with two hostages?"

"I doubt it," McKernan answered grimly.

The time seemed to crawl until Chen radioed that he was in position. He'd sent Ferris out to the end of corridor C to fetch the helmet of his surface suit just in case. When they showed up he had set them to checking the five remaining huts in the section but they had turned up empty.

"Sir, Chen just called in," came Cox's voice over the comm. "He's at the airlock and waiting."

"Thanks. We're about ready to go in," McKernan said.

"OK. Gaeretts, you take the left side, I'll take the right. Ferris, you stay in the lock and cover us. Shorter and Kaminski, you stay put in the corridor. Ready?"

They all nodded assent.

Gently McKernan reopened the outer door of the lock. He motioned to Gaeretts to turn off the airlock's overhead light. The lock control panel showed that the hut was at the same pressure as the corridor. As quietly as he could, he undogged the inner hatch. He drew his revolver. Gaeretts and Ferris had their pistols at the ready. With his fingers McKernan counted down from three and threw the hatch open. The length of the hut was in darkness.

He and Gaeretts pushed inside moving to opposite sides of the hut. Frozen for a second, they listened. There was nothing to hear.

There was just enough light bleeding in from the corridor through the airlock hatch for them to make their way. Slowly they edged forward. The hut wasn't completely empty. The floor was littered with pieces of detritus, the remnants of former uses that weren't worth scavenging. In the dark, it made the footing treacherous.

They reached the first bulkhead, a thin sheet of reinforced metal that formed part of the structure of the hut. An opening about three meters wide pierced its center. The two policemen edged through it. If anything, this new section was darker than the first.

They moved forward, sliding their feet silently along, feeling their way. McKernan's foot contacted something soft and yielding. Reaching down in the darkness he could feel human flesh, not yet cold. It was a leg. Thoughts raced though his mind. Were they too late for Ortiz?

He turned on his flash, waving the narrow beam over the body. It was a woman, not Ortiz, dressed in a short, thin dress. The bruising of strangulation showed at her neck; another victim of Buche. McKernan assumed it was the Dolores that had called Ortiz.

They stood over the body for a moment, thankful it wasn't Constable Ortiz, but aware of what it might mean for her fate.

Gaeretts played the beam of his flashlight over the darkened section. It fastened on a bank of switches attached to the bulkhead. He looked questioningly at his superior. McKernan nodded. At this point, Buche must be aware of their presence.

One by one Gaeretts worked the switches, and with each switch a portion of the overhead lighting flickered on. In the harsh light, the body at McKernan's feet looked pitiful, a small broken thing lying in the dust and debris of the hut's floor.

Gaeretts peered around the edge of the bulkhead into the last section of the hut. It was as barren as the other two had been, but at the far end of the room to one side of the cargo lock that occupied most of the far wall, was a small space fitted out as an office with a window looking out into the hut. Through that window they could see movement.

Buche stepped out of the office holding Ortiz in front of him as a shield, his left arm firmly around her, his right holding an efficient looking knife to her throat.

"Stay where you are. Don't take another step forward or I kill the constable."

"Don't do anything foolish, Buche. We've got you surrounded."

CHAPTER 33: STALEMATE

So it's come down to this, McKernan thought irreverently, two men with weapons shouting clichés at each other over a distance of twenty paces.

"Buche, don't make things any worse than they are. Let the constable go. There's no way for you to get away. There's nowhere for you to go. This is Mars."

"Mars. What a rotten place, eh?" Buche said with a terse laugh. His voice still retained a strong French-Canadian accent. " I should have stayed on Earth."

"Let the constable go, Buche, and I'll see to it that you get sent back to Earth," McKernan said, trying to voice a sympathy he didn't feel.

"What, to a prison? That's no way for a man like me to live, policeman."

"No, Buche. Not a prison. A hospital. You need help. I'll see that you get it."

"A hospital? You mean a loony bin. What do you know about it, Mr. Inspector? Oh, I know who you are, Chief Inspector McKernan. You think you are so smart, so tough. But you know nothing about tough."

McKernan was thinking desperately about how to handle the situation. He wasn't experienced in handling the insane. Drunks, yes, but not crazy knife wielding homicidal maniacs. And it was quite clear that Buche was insane. But how was he to talk a crazy man into releasing his hostage?

He could see the wild glint in Buche's eyes. Push too hard and the knife he held would slice into Ortiz's throat. There was fear in the eyes of the constable, but something else, too. Faith, faith in him, McKernan, that somehow he would find a way out of this situation.

Slowly McKernan lowered his gun and motioned to Gaeretts and Ferris to do the same. When the lights had come on, the latter had moved up so that he was standing just behind the opening in the bulkhead.

"Maybe I don't understand, Buche. Why don't you explain it to me. Why did you have to kill those women?"

The question seemed to puzzle Buche. He stood uncertainly, his gaze flicking between the three policemen facing him.

"They weren't women, McKernan. They were lies. All lies and dirty whores. The priests back in Quebec used to warn us about painted women. About avoiding the temptations of the flesh. They were right. I should have listened to them and stayed in Canada. On Earth."

"You can go back, Buche. Back where you can breathe the air. Back where the sky is blue and the ground is covered in green. Just let the constable go."

Buche seemed to waver for a moment, then he straightened up.

"It's too late for that, Inspector. I've been polluted. This rotten world has polluted my soul and I can never go back."

"That's not true, Pierre Buche. You can get therapy. Even absolution." McKernan wasn't sure about the last, theology had never been one of his strengths. All he knew, is that the longer he kept Buche talking, the more likely that Ortiz might survive.

A flicker of hope crossed Buche's face, then he shook his head.

"You know, Inspector. The first one, she wasn't even a woman. I'd been OK up to then, still pure. But that first one, she looked like a little girl with her yellow hair and skinny body. But she wasn't a little girl. She was a little boy under that dress, something to tempt me with. When I found out, when I felt her stiffen between her legs, I squeezed. I squeezed until she was dead. Then I hid her underneath the floor in the corridor. And I ran."

"He wasn't dead, Buche. Just unconscious. But he died from the cold. He'd never wanted to come to Mars in the first place."

"I tell you something, Inspector, something I never tell anyone. There was a man, a priest, when I was a boy. People said things about him, but no one ever did anything." Buche was almost sobbing. "When I was twelve, no eleven, he got me alone once, in the school. I knew what he wanted, but he was bigger than me, stronger. He put his hands on me, spoke softly saying it was God's will. But I knew he was lying. I got my hands around his throat and I squeezed until he let me go. Then he slapped me and said how I had wanted it, how he could tell. But I didn't. I swear I didn't."

"That wasn't your fault, Buche. You didn't do anything wrong."

"They kicked me out of that school. The priest, they sent him to another parish. I never heard what happened to him after that."

Buche's eyes seemed to lose their focus for a second. That was dangerous. McKernan wanted to keep him talking.

"Why did you kill Lola, Buche?"

"After the girl who was a boy, I tried to ignore women. I tried to live pure. But that Lola, she was a whore, and she tried to tempt me. I tried to ignore her, but she kept after me, so I beat her up."

"But why did you kill her?"

"The next time I came to Hut Town she had changed her hair. It was dyed the same color as the boy's. I couldn't take that. So I waited to catch her in the airlock and I grabbed her and choked her and hid her body so she couldn't tempt me again."

"And Mary?"

"Does it matter? She was the one dyeing peoples hair. Besides, I heard she had been talking to the constable, here. So I killed her to keep her from talking about me."

"What about Dolores, Buche? What did she do to you?"

"She was just another whore. I killed her. That's all." McKernan could sense that Buche had reached the point where he wouldn't talk much longer.

"The time for killing has stopped, Buche," McKernan said with sadness. "Let the constable go. No harm will come to you. I promise. You'll get sent back to Earth where they will be able to help you."

"No. No Earth for me," Buche said with resignation. "But you're right. It's time for the killing to stop."

He started to move towards the hatch of the cargo airlock in the end wall of the hut. Ortiz's eyes widened in realization.

"Buche, stop. I can't let you go. You know that, don't you?"

"Don't come near me, Inspector, or I kill the constable."

Buche had backed up against the control panel for the airlock. Using his elbow, he pushed the large red button that opened the inner hatch. Slowly, the big door began to open, swinging ponderously up to reveal the inside of the lock.

"Buche. It won't work. You can't get away. You don't have your helmet on."

"I know," Buche said slowly, almost regretfully. "It's time to end it."

"Then just let the constable go. I won't try to interfere. You have my word," McKernan shouted desperately.

"No. Without the constable, you'll try to stop me."

"I can't let you take her, Buche," McKernan said raising his revolver. Gaeretts and Ferris had their pistols up, too, but the 5 mm automatics were not very accurate at twenty meters.

The big lock door was wide open now and Buche backed slowly into the lock, Ortiz held in front of him as a shield. He was only a few steps from the interior controls.

"Stop, Buche, or I'll have to shoot. I have no choice."

"We all have choices, Inspector. I've made mine."

"Don't touch that control panel. I'll shoot."

"You won't shoot. You might hit the constable." Buche reached out and hit the button to close the hatch.

"Let her go, Buche," McKernan cried, the heavy revolver held before him. He could only see a portion of Buche's head above Ortiz.

"Take the shot, sir," Ortiz said quietly.

The hatch was swinging shut. McKernan squeezed the trigger of his gun. The shot boomed in the metallic confines of the empty hut. McKernan rushed forward while the hatch continued to close.

"Stop that damned door," McKernan shouted. Gaeretts reached the control panel and slammed the button. The hatch stopped and then reversed itself.

Buche had slumped to the floor of the hatch, a hole in the middle of his forehead. The outer hatch behind him was splattered with brains and blood. Ortiz was still standing, looking pale.

There was a thin whistle of air coming from the hole that McKernan's bullet had made in the outer hatch.

"Ferris, find something to plug that damned hole," the Inspector shouted as he reached for Ortiz.

"Are you ok, Constable?"

"I think you'd better call the doctor, sir," Ortiz said, smiling. "I think I'm going to have the baby. Now."

"Gaeretts, you heard the lady, I think you'd better call the doctor."

Chapter 34: Epilogue

It was nearly a day later before McKernan finally had a chance to look in on Constable Ortiz at the hospital. First there had been the business of getting Ortiz to the hospital, no easy task, considering that she had made her announcement at what was possibly the point in Hut Town most remote from medical services. After a hurried consultation with Dr. Haestert, McKernan and Gaeretts had escorted her down Corridor B until they were met by the doctor and a wheel-chair. Ortiz had protested that she didn't need the chair until a contraction convinced her otherwise.

With the constable in competent medical hands, the inspector had returned to deal with the crime scene to supervise the necessary collection of evidence not only for the shooting of Buche but also for the demise of the hapless Dolores. The investigation revealed signs that Buche had, in fact, been intermittently camping out in the office area of the hut for months if not longer. He had stocked it with enough supplies to have lasted him a month. The adjacent restroom had served for his sanitary needs.

It was well past 0300 by the time the bodies had been removed and the evidence secured, allowing the inspector a scant four hours to finish his preliminary report of the "Buche incident." This was completed just in time for McKernan to endure a two hour lecture by the Trust Authority governor about how he had made a total mess of the entire situation, a mess that would leave an indelible black mark on the record of the governor's administration on Mars, an administration that fortunately was coming to an end with his imminent reassignment to a much more pleasant posting on Earth. It was only this latter fact that had convinced the governor not to ask for McKernan's immediate resignation.

After the dressing down by the governor, McKernan's enquiries at the hospital had revealed that Ortiz was doing fine but still in labor. Realizing that it had been some thirty two hours since he had slept, the inspector faced the inevitable and went home.

It was therefore not until 1800 that he made his appearance at the hospital.

"How's she doing, Beth?" were the first words out of his mouth when he stepped through the hatch into the hospital lobby.

Dr. Haestert, who looked as worn out as he had felt six hours earlier smiled as she answered, "She and little Miguel are doing fine. She's resting now. You can see her for a moment if you like."

"Good. There weren't any problems?"

"Considering it was her first pregnancy, no. Constable Ortiz is a remarkably sturdy woman. Still, she was in labor for nearly twenty hours. That takes a lot out of a person, so you'll have to keep your visit brief. And no excitement."

"I think we've both had enough of that for the moment," McKernan said with a sigh.

The doctor's expression echoed McKernan's sentiment. "It's really over now, Erik, isn't it? I mean with Buche. I've been so busy that I haven't heard all the details."

"Yes, it's really over. Buche is dead, and I prevented him from adding Ortiz to the list of his victims."

"Four people murdered. It seems hard to believe. I thought crime was one thing I was getting away from by coming to Mars."

"Buche should never have made it through the screening process, but somehow he did. But you have to wonder if any of this would have happened if Guzman's father hadn't shipped him off to Mars."

"That still bothers me, the thought of that poor boy freezing to death alone in that tunnel," the doctor said with a shudder.

"It's time to put the whole business behind us. Can I see Ortiz now."

"OK. But only for a minute." She escorted the inspector into the bay where Ortiz lay resting, the baby cradled in her arms.

As he entered, the constable smiled proudly up at him. "I'm a momma."

"So you are, Constable."

"I'd offer you a seat, but I'm afraid Mike is taking that up," she nodded at the man sleeping in the chair next to her bed. "When he heard I was in labor, he and a friend drove all the way from Junction 3. He got here just in time to see the delivery. Then he fell asleep."

"I envy him," McKernan commented. "Are you all right? You've been through a lot."

"I'm fine, sir. I'll be ready to go back to patrol as soon as the doctor says it's ok."

"You're sure? I'd understand. And you've got the baby, now."

"I'm sure, sir. I'm a policeman. It's what I do. Mike and I have already talked about it, when I first found out I was pregnant. We can manage. Jenny said she'll be happy to help out with the Miguel when I'm out on patrol."

"Well, we can talk about this later. Right now you need your rest."

"Sir?," Ortiz said hesitatingly. "I know what I did was a boneheaded move."

"It was stupid and dangerous, constable."

"I know. It's just that I felt responsible. I didn't want Buche to kill anyone else because of me. When Dolores called me, she sounded scared. She said she knew where Buche was hiding, but she didn't want to talk to anybody but me because of what happened to Mary. I believed her. Buche must have known, though, because he ambushed me as I was going to the meeting place."

It struck McKernan that Ortiz didn't know yet that Buche had killed Dolores after he had made her call the constable. The body had been hidden by the dark in the hut. He saw no point in telling Ortiz about that at the moment. There would be time enough for that later.

"It was a dumb stunt, Ortiz, but I'd probably have done the same thing in your place. Just don't do it again. Deal?"

"Deal, sir."

"Good, get some sleep, now. Doctor's orders."

Beth was waiting outside the patient bay when he was done. "Everything ok? With you and Ortiz, I mean. I've heard bits and pieces about what happened."

"Yeah, we're good," McKernan answered wryly.

"I'm glad. Look, I'm about done here. I wouldn't mind going for a drink. I could use one."

"That's the best thing I've heard today," McKernan said with a smile.

Author's Afterword

A Corpse in Hut Town is the third novel to feature Chief Inspector McKernan, following *The Blood Red Sands of Mars* and *A Death at Station Alpha*. While the first of these, *Blood Red Sands*, is actually more of an action/thriller sort of story than a true mystery, *A Death at Station Alpha* was modeled from the beginning on the English country house mystery with an isolated research station taking the place of the country house. Taking yet another turn, *A Corpse in Hut Town* is essentially a police procedural, with McKernan and his department trying to track down a serial killer while having to work within the limited forensic capabilities of available on Mars.

The inspiration for this novel comes from what must be one of the most curious unsolved mysteries in the history of Madison, Wisconsin. In 1989, workers doing some repairs to the chimney of a music store discovered the remains of what at first appeared to be a young woman. The body had been there some time and both the body and clothing had undergone considerable deterioration. Everyone involved with the investigation was surprised when an autopsy revealed that the body was actually that of a young man. As of this date, nearly two decades after the discovery, not only does the murder remain unsolved, but the identity of the victim has never been determined.

While considering ideas for a third "Murder on Mars" book I had been drawn to the idea of McKernan having to track down a serial killer through the corridors of Hut Town, the labyrinth of pneumatic architecture left over from the earliest days of Martian exploration. Having been in Madison during the flurry of press coverage that followed the discovery of the body in the chimney, it was only natural that a similar situation should serve as the jumping off point for the story.

For those who have read *A Death at Station Alpha*, Constable Elena Ortiz, the character I introduced in that book, returns playing a much more active role. *A Corpse in Hut Town* takes place roughly a year after *Station Alpha*, and Ortiz has made the decision to remain on Mars, has settled down with her boyfriend Mike, a mechanic at Junction 3, and is, as they say, "in a family way."

As with the first two books in the series, not only have I tried to write an entertaining story, but I have also used the novel to explore the difficulties and possibilities presented by the settlement of another planet. In particular, Hut Town, which operates outside the auspices of both the Trust Authority and the corporations, has been fleshed out in more detail than either of the previous two books. While I have read extensively about the exploration of Mars almost from the time I could first read, the ideas in this series are strictly my own and I freely admit that reality has been twisted in places for dramatic effect.

I hope you enjoyed this book. If you did, I hope you will read the other two books if you have not already done so. And, yes, I am already working on a concept for the next book in the series which is tentatively to be entitled *Murder at the Mars Club*.

Greg Fowlkes
January 18, 2014

The Blood Red Sands of Mars

The wind was blowing again against the west wall of the hut. He could hear the grains of sand abrading the thin aluminum skin that protected him from the outside. Through the window, half frosted from the continuous onslaught of sand and dust, he could see clouds of dust obscuring the sky. The sky was a pastel pink, a color no sky had any right to be. The wind, despite its 120 kph. velocity, made only a thin howl as it blew over the half buried cylinder of the hut.

McKernan lay on his cot trying not to admit that he was awake. It was a losing battle. After a few minutes he surrendered and glanced over at the clock sitting on the crate next to his bed. The dim red digits of the LED display read 7:58. It was too early to get up, too late to go back to sleep. He rolled over, shivering at the cold. The temperature couldn't have been more than ten degrees Celsius inside the hut. For the twentieth time he thought to himself that he would have to fix the heater before winter—if he could get the parts. Either that, or put in more insulation—if he could find that. The cold finally forced the decision to get up.

Standing, he felt the cold plastic floor beneath his bare feet. With his foot he fished the worn and patched pants from beneath the cot and pulled them on. He dug underneath his pillow and came up with a switchblade knife that he stuck in his pocket before drawing on the turtleneck sweater that had lain next to his pants. The cold feel of the cloth did nothing to dispel the cold from his body. From the crate he picked up a shoulder holster with a small automatic pistol and put it on. McKernan drew the weapon, worked the slide once, and after examining it perfunctorily, placed it back in the holster. Satisfied, he pulled on a worn pair of leather boots and placed another knife in a sheathe between his skin and the boot top.

Dressed, he went over to the shelf that served as counter and table. He put a pan of beans onto the heating unit and got a soysteak from the small refrigerator that held up one end of the shelf. The steak went into the frying pan on the other heating element. An egg would have been nice, but at the current price of three dollars apiece it was an extravagance that he would have to put off for a while.

As the food cooked he drew a liter of water from the spigot in the corner of the hut and watered the plants in the garden under the window. The carrots and tomatoes were doing nicely. He smiled briefly because it would be good to have fresh vegetables for a change. The big, leafy oxygen plants were doing well, too. He would be able to cut down on his oxygen ration this month and save some money.

He took the beans off the heating element and replaced them with the coffee pot. The beans were still half cold, but he wasn't in the mood to hassle with them. He only had the two heating elements, and he didn't want to have to wait for his coffee. He forced down the beans and then wolfed down the steak. It almost tasted like real beef, but then maybe his memories were fading. As usual, the coffee tasted terrible and tepid, too. The air pressure in the hut was too low for water to boil properly.

He finished his meal and scraped the remnants of food into the pressure vessel that served as a compost heap. The gauge on its neighbor showed that he had almost half a tank of methane. He'd be able to sell that soon and use the money for something useful, like a still. Completing his rounds, the gauges on the life support systems showed that everything was still working at keeping him alive. He went back to the pots and scrubbed them clean with sand. That, at least, was plentiful and cheap.

He checked his watch against the clock. It was time to get going. Pulling on his jacket he went to the airlock at the corridor end of the hut. After checking the gauge to make sure that there was pressure on the other side, he undogged the latches and stepped through. Closing the door behind him, he repeated the process with the outer hatch, latching both doors behind him. The outer door he locked with a heavy padlock.

He had entered a low tubular corridor made of the same aluminum foil and plastic foam construction as the hut. The walls, however, were even thinner, and no pretense was made of heating it. He could see his breath condensing in front of him as he began to walk down its length. It was a hell of a way to live, he reflected, not for the first time. But then, it had been hell living in L.A. where he'd been born, with brown air, rats, a chronic shortage of water, and overcrowded tenements. He had made his choice, but sometimes it seemed as though life was a continual shiver.

The corridor was pierced at regular intervals by hatches identical to his own. The huts behind the hatches were identical, too, except for the modifications the owners had made to make them more livable. This part of the city was old, dating back a couple of decades to the first days of the settlement when it had been part of a scientific base. The scientists had departed, at least from that corridor, and been replaced by those who had the money to buy or rent the huts from the Trust Authority. Maintenance was pretty much left up to the residents.

Along the sides and overhead ran the pipes and conduits that pumped in the gases, liquids, and power necessary for sustaining life. The whole system looked as jury rigged and fragile as it actually was, though surprisingly few people died whenever the system failed. Martians were a cautious lot. One didn't talk much about injuries. Accidents on Mars didn't leave many.

A hundred meters down the tube he came to an airlock. Going through the same ritual that he had used on his front door, he went through to another length of corridor indistinguishable from the one he had just left. Continuing on, he passed through two more airlocks until he entered a corridor that sloped downward. The hatches were farther apart, and larger. Signs overhead indicated the businesses or functions that were carried out behind them. The air was warmer because the corridor was buried beneath the sand which provided insulation. At the end of the tunnel was a larger airlock set into a wall of fused silica bricks, the first substantial piece of construction he had met that morning.

Passing through the portal was like entering another world, which in a way he had. This was the public Mars, the planet seen by the corporation men and the officials of the Trust Authority. It was also the planet seen by tourists, the brave new colony, man's first outpost on another planet. The tourists didn't really care to see the hut town. They were part of the same world as the corporation men and the government types. It still took a great deal of money or power to reach Mars.

The difference was more than one of degree. For one thing, the temperature was a comfortable twenty. For another, the walls were flat and met the floors and ceilings at right angles, unlike the inflated skins of the huts and corridors. With a little imagination it could almost be an enclosed shopping mall on earth, though the presence of fused silica blocks was more prevalent than any architect would allow.

The most important difference, however, was the sight of people scurrying along. He hadn't met anyone in the outer corridors. People rarely lingered there because of the cold. Now, McKernan could see at least twenty people and it was still fairly early. No airlocks interrupted this corridor. Extending for two hundred meters in either direction, it was twenty meters wide and ten high, the largest enclosed volume on the planet. Arrayed along its length were the offices and store fronts of the corporations that owned Mars, as well as the more prosperous saloons and bordellos.

One day the Trust Authority promised that the whole city would be like that, with apartments and condominiums for the ordinary workers, but neither the Authority or the corporations had yet come up with the money. For the moment all that existed was the one street of a few blocks.

McKernan headed towards the Authority's offices which dominated one end of the mall, but turned aside at the last moment when he noticed that a small, dark doorway was open. He knew that he should resist the temptation, but he was not in a very disciplined mood. He went through the doorway into the darkness beyond.

Finnegan's was the only real, honest bar on Mars. There were any number of saloons and even a cocktail lounge in the Mars Sheraton, but only one quiet, dark place where a man could drink in peace. McKernan felt the need for some of that peace at the moment.

He sat down on one of the stools before the only mahogany bar on Mars. Finnegan, himself, was behind the bar, though in fact he almost always was, no matter what the hour. The bartender looked up and greeted the newcomer, "Good morning, Constable. Beer or whiskey?"

"It's too early for beer. It's too early for whiskey, but give me a shot, anyway."

Finnegan poured out a shot glass of amber liquid and placed it before McKernan and then stood back polishing a glass while he studied the man opposite him.

McKernan knocked back half the glass before he spoke. When he did, there was a bitter edge to his voice. "Sometimes I wonder if it's worth it, Finnegan. I could be back on a planet fit for human life."

"Could you, now, Constable?" Finnegan said, putting down the glass and picking up another in equally gleaming condition. "If mother earth was such a bed of roses, why are you here?"

He breathed on the glass and examined it against the light for a moment, then looked at McKernan with the same intentness. "You're here because you're not the sort to live off the dole or to spend your life with another man being your boss. Instead you'll spend your life trying to make this planet a fit place to live and retire in twenty years with a nice pension. Now drink up and get to work, laddy."

"Yeah, sure. Sorry to burden you with my problems. Early morning depression, I guess. See you." He finished off the shot and left five dollars in Authority script on the bar.

The bite of the whiskey so early in the morning didn't really help his disposition, but it did give him enough courage to make it to the office. The morning ritual at Finnegan's was becoming too much of a habit. His three years on Mars were beginning to show.

The jail wasn't in the brick part of the Authority building, but in the complex of pneumatic architecture that sprawled behind it. The huts were old—older than his own—but dated back to the days when governments had not begrudged a few billions for exploration, back before space had to show a profit. For that reason, they were sound and well insulated, though a bit tacky looking.

The jail consisted of two huts joined together, one for offices, the other for the two makeshift cells and storage. Ferris was the only one there when he walked in, a young kid, younger than he had been himself when he had come to Mars. He was still impressed enough with his responsibilities and had not yet been worn down by the grim realities to take his job in any way but seriously.

Ferris greeted him with a solemn, "Good morning, sir," with a stress on the sir. As a three year veteran of Mars, Ferris looked on his boss with more than a touch of awe.

"Anything exciting happen overnight?" McKernan didn't really expect much. A few fights in the saloon district, a knifing maybe if things got out of hand. Petty thievery, or perhaps not so petty. He looked at Ferris and saw a flash of excitement in his eyes that the younger man was trying hard to suppress in order to match the hard bitten image he had of his superior.

"Yes, sir. We've got a murder on our hands."

"Another knifing down at Thelma's?" he asked, naming an infamous saloon and bordello that figured in a quarter of all the police reports.

"No. A prospector was found out on his claim yesterday, over on the far side of Olympus Mons. He was shot, Inspector."

That was bad, McKernan thought. People on Mars weren't supposed to have guns. With the thin skins of most buildings and a hostile atmosphere outside that would support life exactly as long as you could hold your breath, they were dangerous, and not just to the targets. The Authority had made them illegal and the corporations had been more than willing to agree. They weren't easy to get—not something that could be picked up casually or made, like a knife. Even without the details it sounded like the work of a real criminal and not just a squabble over a claim or a woman.

"Okay. Let me have the report. I'll take a look at it."

He took the folder from Ferris who looked a bit crestfallen. He probably expects me to go rush off to the outside and track down the murderer like an Indian scout, McKernan thought. He'd learn in time. Mars was a big planet and a dangerous one, but because of its nature there were also very few places that a man could run to and none where he could hide indefinitely.

He was leafing through the report when he came to his door. For the thousandth time he read, "Inspector Erik McKernan, Chief Constable." Mother would have been proud, he thought sardonically. She had hated the L.A. cops like all the other residents of the barrio. He went through the door into the little cubicle that was his real home. There, sitting at his desk, he began to read the report, sketchy though it was, to look for some explanations.

The Fictional Press
www.TheFictionalPress.com

About The Fictional Press

The Fictional Press, an imprint of Intrepid Ink, LLC, provides full publishing services to authors of fiction and non-fiction books, eBooks and websites. From editing to formatting, to publishing, to marketing, Intrepid Ink gets your creative works into the hands of the people who want to read them.

Find out more at www.thefictionalpress.com.

www.ingramcontent.com/pod-product-compliance
Lightning Source LLC
Chambersburg PA
CBHW071324250626
47159CB00004B/1452

* 9 7 8 1 9 3 7 0 2 2 6 7 9 *